FIGHTING IT

Regi Claire

TWO RAVENS
PRESS

Published by Two Ravens Press Ltd.
Green Willow Croft
Rhiroy
Lochbroom
Ullapool
Ross-shire IV23 2SF

www.tworavenspress.com

ISBN: 978-1-906120-41-2

British Library Cataloguing in Publication Data: a CIP record for this book can be obtained from the British Library.

Designed and typeset in Sabon by Two Ravens Press.
Cover design by David Knowles and Sharon Blackie.
Cover image © Pac, Agency Dreamstime.com

Printed on Forest Stewardship Council-accredited paper by the MPG books group.

Mixed Sources
Product group from well-managed forests, controlled sources and recycled wood or fiber
www.fsc.org   Cert no. TT-COC-002303
© 1996 Forest Stewardship Council
FSC

The publisher gratefully acknowledges subsidy from the Scottish Arts Council towards the publication of this volume.

Scottish
Arts Council

About the Author

Born and brought up in Switzerland, Regi Claire now lives in Edinburgh with her husband, the writer Ron Butlin, and their golden retriever. Her mother tongue is Swiss German, but she writes in English. Her previous books are *Inside~Outside* (shortlisted for the Saltire First Book Award) and *The Beauty Room* (longlisted for the MIND Book of the Year Award). Her work has appeared in many literary magazines and anthologies (including *Cleave* from Two Ravens Press), also in translation and on BBC Radio 4. She won *The Edinburgh Review* 10th Anniversary Short Story Competition, was a *Cadenza* prize winner, and has received Bursaries from the Scottish Arts Council, Pro Helvetia and Thurgau Lottery Foundation, as well as a UBS Cultural Foundation Award. She is a creative writing tutor at the National Gallery of Scotland.

For more information about the author, see
www.tworavenspress.com

Acknowledgements

Some of the stories in this collection first appeared, in earlier form, in *Cadenza* 7, *Chapman* 102-103, *Cleave: New Writing by Women in Scotland* (Two Ravens Press), *Dreams That Money Can Buy* 3, *Edinburgh Review* 109, 117 ('Because You Foreign', published as 'No Volcano, Goddammit. No Smoke Holes') and 126, *Familia* 7-8 (Romania), *Northwords* 30 ('Smell the Roses', published as 'The Legacy'), *ONE Magazine* 5, *Sandstone Review* 9, on the website of the Scottish Arts Council, in *Scottish Book Collector* 7:10, *Stolen Stories* (Forest Publications), *Tears in the Fence* 43, *Textualities* 1 ('Everybody Goes Crazy Once in While', published as 'Patchouli, Loulou and Opium') and in *Word Jig: New Fiction From Scotland* (New York: Hanging Loose Press).

'Cool Room 3' was also broadcast on BBC Radio 4 and was *The Guardian*'s Radio Pick of the Day.

Many thanks to Sharon Blackie and David Knowles at TRP, to my agent Lucy Luck, and to Louise Welsh. Thank you also to Ernst Ammann, Mark Bailey, Senay Boztas, Marie Bremner and Roger Quin, Karen and Simon Brown, Maria Campbell, Sarah Carpenter and Randall Stevenson, Dorothy and Mike Cloughley, Karen Clulow, Judy and Stewart Conn, Catherine and Lyell Cresswell, Graham Cumberland, Sean Doyle, Francesca Dymond and Steve McNicoll, Thomas and Pascal Egli, Lesley Glaister, Joyce Gunn Cairns, Louise and Ed Harper, Dorothy and Sally Harrower, Elaine Henry and Tarlochan Gata-Aura, Barbara Imrie and Louis Gillespie, Pauline Jones and Gavin Wallace, Kath Latham and Donald Howitt, Sabine Lehner, Sue Liebermann, Kevin Lowrie, Carmen Mäder, Robyn Marsack, Iain Matheson, Béatrice and Malcolm McCallum, Linda and John McClelland, Reuben Merrick, Susan Nickalls, Liz Niven, Anthony Pilley, Julie and Tom Pow, Ursi Ross and Edinburgh Swiss Club/ Swiss Benevolent Fund Scotland, Marlis Rüegger, Dorli Ryf, Rose Sawkins, Linda Scotland, Hazel Sheppard, Waki and Nigel Smith, Angela and Martin Staub, Paul-Edwin Staub, Zoe Strachan, Pam Thomson and Thomas Spencer, Valerie Thornton, Käthi Wuffli, and to all my other friends for helping me to 'fight it'. A special thank you to Ron and my parents – for everything.

For Wiebke Abel, Lel and Robin Blair (and Guinevere!), Marion Campbell, Lynda Clark and Richard Mowe, Agnès and Roland Dannreuther, Catherine Durandard, Marianne-Vera and Rahel Egli, Ruth Gruber, Jutta and Christoph Lischer, Sian Mackay, Stella and Patrick Rayner, Dora and Lucas Staub, and, of course, Ron.

Contents

Introduction

Fighting It   1
Cool Room 3   16
Russian Blue   24
The Death Queue   34
I Call Her Salome   44
Invisible Partners   59
'Because You Foreign'   68
Diessenhofen Bridge   78
Heat   87
The Punishment   97
Snow White and the Prince   105
Smell the Roses   115
Everybody Goes Crazy Once in a While   122
Meeting the Exiled Emperor   132
Walking Down the Line   139
The Marilyn Monroe of the Meadows   154

Introduction

by Louise Welsh

I have a small collection of globes of the world. They show oceans charted and uncharted, and countries that, though formed around familiar borders, vary in proportion depending on which globe you consult. My largest one, the modern version stamped Made in China that doubles as a lamp, depicts Britain as a tiny state not much bigger than my thumbnail, while the small, tin 1950s ex-classroom globe that presents the empire in pale pink (why pink?) has swollen Britain to almost half the size of America. They look good together, these various versions of the world, but I don't trust them. It seems to me that each of the geographers had their own agenda. But perhaps I'm being too cynical. After all, it's hard to see the space we inhabit, to picture the world, hold it in your hands and find it right.

Regi Claire's new collection *Fighting It* captures many worlds within its slim bounds. They too differ widely from each other, but I trust their integrity much more than the distorted versions that decorate my assortment of globes. Some of Claire's societies are rarefied. In 'Heat', Nicole Müller is part of a set where tennis lessons, scented rose gardens and thoroughbred horses blunt the edges of boredom. Others occupy territory more familiar to most of us; Michelle's Borders cottage in 'Everybody Goes Crazy Once in a While' or the route of Bonnie and Heather's walk in 'Marilyn Monroe of the Meadows'.

The locations of these stories range across Britain, Europe and beyond. 'Sorry about the racket Mum' shouts Rosa/Rosie Harrower's son down the telephone line in 'Invisible Partners', 'I'm in the middle of the Amazon rainforest. How are you?' But this is no travelogue and although Claire is as confident evoking, among other places, her native Switzerland, a French Embassy in a small Middle East Kingdom or a well-kent hill in

Edinburgh where she currently lives, it's not merely the scope of her settings that grant the sense of a realised world. It's her crafting of a wealth of characters that ultimately manages to capture the variety and complexity of the lives around us.

Laura, the anti-hero of the title story, is haunted by the very acts that fuel her fantasies. She tries to damp down her urges with exercise, allowing herself one indulgence, one other life, her cat Bandit. But Laura is only ever a thought away from brutality and the rhythm of her feet against the treadmill as she runs adds a percussive sense of tension to her struggle with the system and her own sadistic urges. The difficulties confronting Claire's protagonists are not always so dramatic, but they are all fighting something.

Under pressure some individuals behave counter to their own interests. Young Cathy commits a seemingly illogical act of destruction in 'The Punishment'. The nameless narrator in 'The Death Queue' drifts through her dwindling stock of days more jealous of her already dead love than she is of the living. And Max Gruber of 'Cool Room 3' too easily abandons his life at the side of the road. The conviction that she made a dreadful decision when she was a young woman has blighted the existence of Alice in 'Snow White and the Prince'. But is this belief as perverse as the urge that prompted her resolution all those years ago?

Fighting It suggests worlds where choices can be made, though sometimes the options available come from a poor and dwindled stock. Laura can decide which library books she reads, but not the fancies they invoke. Michelle can force a major life change, but has no control over her neighbours' reactions. On a day when a terrorist attack invades faraway London Max Gruber, safe in Switzerland, begins to think he has made a series of wrong choices, but will a sudden whim improve his existence or devastate it?

The stories in *Fighting It* are so finely wrought that it can be a surprise to realise how short some of them are. These are whole universes captured in a drop of water. Claire allows us access into the heart of lives and people unmet. And even though we may be very different from the individuals we encounter between these pages, we can gain a moment of shared humanity with them. Not simply because Regi Claire grants us privileged access to their worlds and psyches but because we are all up against something and every one of us fighting it, *Fighting It*.

This is a truly fabulous collection.

Fighting It

She was in the wire cage again, exercising like a rat in the wheel. The late summer sun glared down into the yard, and most of the other women drooped in heaps on benches or lay sprawled on the grassy oval in the centre, dozing.

Stamp-stamp-stamp went Laura's feet. The wire cage had been erected next to one of the tall surrounding walls, in the shade of a beech tree. The handrail was slick with sweat. Sweat runnelled down her cleavage, slithered over her stomach, greased her back. It dripped from the blonde stubble on her head, swamped her eyes. She wasn't wearing any jewellery, not even her ear studs or the nose ring. They'd taken those away from her – just in case.

Glancing around the yard for an instant, Laura caught sight of a thin figure shambling about at the far end. A figure that reminded her of someone from Outside. But the face was turned away so she couldn't be sure. Maybe it was a mirage; the sun was harsh and hot enough for that. She grimaced, then wiped the sweat from her eyes and concentrated on the workout.

Her black trainers were blurs on the treadmill. She'd cranked up the incline to 9% and upped the speed from the previous day. With hypnotic regularity the red numbers of the LED display flipped from running time to distance to running time ... until they became meaningless smears.

Stamp-stamp-stamp went her feet, deep inside an imaginary forest. The pine needles on the floor were the colour of a fox's pelt and their springiness bounced her on and on through the warm, woody air. The scent of resin was all around her. She felt cocooned within its golden transparency. Safe. It seemed to preserve her as something hard and enduring and – if left alone – quite harmless.

For a moment she felt almost happy.

That was the best Laura could achieve these days: a sensation of almost-ness, and she was careful to treasure it. Not too much and not too little – joy, rage, despair, love, hate. Bandit was her only indulgence. He received the surfeit of her love, never her hate. He was the reason she carried on with the chore of living.

The scent of resin was getting stronger with every stride and there was a rustle of wings now, velvety soft, as two blackbirds joined her, flitting along like shadows conjured from the undergrowth. A squirrel twitched its tail at her, chattering. *No bad thoughts*, it seemed to say. *No bad thoughts*. Sunlight slipped across her cheeks – a caress of sorts.

Stamp-stamp-stamp. Abruptly, the magic forest transformed itself into a sports ground and she was on a cinder track, speeding past other runners every so often. She could see them quite clearly. Smelt them on her very skin. The fat, knock-kneed women with slack mouths and flabby arms, hobbling rather than jogging along. Stupid women, forcing themselves on for the sake of vanity. The kind of women who painted their faces every morning, come rain, come shine. They were the ones she hated most. *Mustn't hate too much, must be wary, stay on an even keel.* Undignified, weak and cowardly they were. Bump into any of them by accident, and there'd be a shriek and a fall. Scared wide puppet eyes would stare up at you...

Oh yes, you know that look – and the raised hands, the sweaty palms. Every night you see them. See the two ghost women crouched at the foot of your bed, one to the left, one to the right, with a gap in the middle where SHE should have been. Their voices rasp like flames over dry wood. They keep asking you something, keep pleading with you. Pleading and asking, they remain crouched there, thick red drops leaking from their bodies. Their pupils getting larger and larger. Their hands still raised. Twitching hands... No, you don't want to see them. No! No!

The red numbers leapt into sudden focus: 5.63 kilometres. Unless Big Martha decided otherwise, she'd do at least five more. Her body was a well-oiled machine. It was the only thing she could trust – apart from Bandit. Laura felt a wave of tenderness wash over her. For a moment she wondered whether she had ever loved anybody as much as him. She'd do anything for him, absolutely anything.

Stamp-stamp-stamp. Placing her hands on the side rails, she lifted her elbows to push herself further, make herself lighter. Soon her arms would turn into wings. Soon she'd be able to fly off and away, wherever she wanted.

But she didn't really want to travel beyond these walls. Didn't really want to leave, full stop. If it was up to her, she'd gladly spend the rest of her life Inside. She'd told them so in court, implored them almost: 'Please don't ever set me free.'

Generally she didn't even want to mix with the others. Much better to stay in her own cell with Bandit. Maybe do a spot of dusting – she took pride in how clean her cell was – some spraying and polishing to let the surfaces flash back the light, and not a single cat hair to mar the reflection. Or she'd browse through her library shelfload of travel guides. Watch TV. Request a session with the live-in psychiatrist – he always welcomed new titbits for the casebook he was writing, on women miso-somethings. Or she might listen to some punk rock on the radio, to get rid of the tension she could feel compressed inside her like so much explosive in a hand grenade. Snatching up Bandit from his basket, she would cradle him in her arms, would fling herself round in time to the beat, shouting and stamping her feet until they were on fire.

You adore fires. Adore the lick of flames, their shivering, greedy feeding. You imagine yourself dancing inside their roar, all the way to oblivion.

Why the hell hadn't they allowed you to become a policewoman? Nothing bad would have happened then. Nothing. Because you'd have ended up on the right side of the law. Instead, thanks to their goddamn rules and regulations, you were branded from the outset. No immigrants, they said. You were born here, for chrissake, wasn't that enough? No criminal record, they said. As if smoking dope and disturbing the peace were crimes! No broken-off apprenticeships, they said. But that wasn't your fault – your first employer's wife, the Schuster woman with her pus-yellow eyes, her hooked nose and sharp, long fingernails, was a number-one bitch.

'Okay?' Big Martha's sallow face hovered centimetres from hers, showing nicotine-stained teeth. There was a pimple on her chin.

The meter said 9.35 kilometres.

Stamp-stamp-stamp went Laura's feet, slower and slower. As she came to a halt, she swept her hands over her head in a quick scissor motion that scattered drops in all directions. Big Martha managed to pull back, though not quite fast enough. Laura grinned innocently, then bent to slap the hard, bunched-up muscles in her thighs and calves. Her black Nike T-shirt, she noted with satisfaction, was drenched.

Straightening up again, she asked: 'You've heard of Nike?'

Big Martha nodded. 'Sure. I got trainers at home.'

Laura just shook her head and smiled. Big Martha was a clod. She'd no idea about goddesses. Or victory.

Before she was let out of the cage, Laura did a quick survey of the yard: the mirage woman had vanished, probably never existed in the first place. *Forget about her. Just forget about her.* She fastened the chains around her ankles and wrists, dutifully, the way they had taught her. Then Big Martha reached in through the specially designed hatch, to double-check. This time Laura's grin was knowing.

So much fear, what a laugh! No therapy will ever chisel away the pleasure you get from people's fear. Beating up those idiot policemen in May was a mistake, of course. They weren't scared of you after all, not even afraid. They were merely doing their job, trying to take you to court. But they needn't have been so damn clumsy about getting you into the van; no wonder you blew your top. One woman against three burly uniforms, for pity's sake!

The workouts are certainly paying off. Still, you've put on six kilos since spring. The food's too good. Six kilos. Why can't they let you starve like in the bad old days? Six bloody kilos. Answer: because they prefer you sluggish and slow, a shifting mass of uncoordinated flesh – a sack of rubbish.

But you won't give in. Won't ever let your body go soft and rotted.

They'd done her cell while she was out. A chemical stink was coming from the toilet and someone's cloth had left careless smears on the gleaming surface of her table. The bedspread she'd so painstakingly smoothed was rucked up near the pillow, with the telltale imprint of a fat arse. Bandit had rolled himself into a ball on top of the wardrobe, his eyes lurid with impotent fury. Usually he met her at the door, purring and preening himself, having been alerted by the familiar clatter of her chains.

'Fuck those slags!'

The Judas window slid open and Big Martha looked in: 'What's the matter?'

'I clean my own fucking place, can't they get that into their stupid heads? Next time Bandit will scratch out their eyes! Tell them that!'

When Big Martha hesitated, Laura banged a fist on the door: 'Piss off!'

Afterwards she smiled to herself; thank Christ they'd leave her in peace now for a while. She undressed, stepped into the shower and let the water reach scalding point. Her skin went pink and blotchy; her scalp started to burn. Finally, she switched to cold. The clash in temperature felt soothing.

As she rubbed herself dry, Laura flicked the bath towel out the shower-room door. 'Hey, Bandit, playtime!'

He streaked down the wardrobe lightning-quick, jumped and bit into the fabric so it snagged on his teeth, then shot off, his rear end fishtailing across the wet tiles.

Laura giggled. By the time she got to him, he was already up on the bedside table and nibbling at the apricots – a present from Coco, the journalist. In between nibbles he seemed to grin at her.

'Wicked boy!' She picked him up and kissed his shiny black nose, touched it with the very tip of her tongue. He miaowed, finished chewing a tiny shred of fruit, then draped himself round her neck, purring and gurgling softly with delight. He felt warm against her chilled skin. Every time he moved, his tail swished over her bare breasts. When he began to lick her left earlobe with precise, sandpapery strokes, she went quite still. She didn't want him to stop. Like a statue she stood in the middle of her cell, one arm lifted to steady him, her face straining sideways, closer to his, while a thrill of affection ran through her. He was flesh and blood. A furry bundle of life. *Her* life.

'Bandit,' she whispered, 'my sweet little Bandit. What would I do without you?'

The newest guidebook she'd borrowed was about the Middle East. Colour pictures of markets with red and orange and yellow spice pyramids, precariously stacked plastic buckets, bowls, drying racks and clocks in the shape of miniature mosques. Oil refineries and pipelines across endless miles of sand. Mirror-glass high-rise towers next to minute palm trees and canals full of toy boats. Camels with single humps. Men in white, baggy trousers, long white shirts and white headscarves fastened with black rods like snakes. Heroes straight out of *Arabian Nights*. The women covered in black. Scurrying scarecrows. Only slits for eyes or some sort of mesh.

You should have become one of them after leaving school. Should have hidden yourself under layers of black. You'd have been invisible. Invincible. A dark shape. A devil in disguise. They wouldn't have caught you then, would they? If every woman was wearing the same outfit, how would they be able to tell who was who? Nothing to identify anybody, except perhaps the shoes. You could have gone about your business unscathed. The anonymous impresario laying on a free spectacle for the masses. A fire here, a fire there. That was later, though. After the women. By then everything was spinning out of control and you were a

6

car without brakes hurtling down a mountainside. And you still are. When you're not on your guard. Fighting it.

Laura pushed the book back into the gap between the guides to Morocco and Argentine on the shelf above her bed. Bandit had curled up on her pillow. Cuddling him with one hand, she ate a couple of the pockmarked apricots. Their flesh had a spongy texture, firm yet yielding, vulnerable with a sweet fragrance that, combined with the downy skin, almost made her retch. She spat the last mouthful into a paper tissue and buried her face in Bandit's fur. She loved to breathe in his clean cat smell; it restored her to herself. His flank rose and fell, rose and fell under her cheek.

After a little while she put on the bedside radio. Started slewing through the stations, round and round, until her finger stopped. Already, she could feel adrenaline pumping through her. Sweat pearled under her arms, on her upper lip, between her breasts. Her heart was racing. Someone seemed to have flipped a switch inside her and she was off again, hurtling down that treacherous, never-ending mountainside.

The music isn't music any longer. Wind instruments snarl at intervals. Snarl-snarl-slash – pause – snarl – pause – slash. Violins scrape, scream, yowl. Whatever the instrument, it must be meant to imitate a knife. You've begun to shake, your hands clench and unclench, then your right slices through the air, flat and precise as a blade.

'Shut up, stupid woman! Shut up! Stupid, STUPID BITCH!'

Two rows of parked cars and a chunky concrete pillar hide you from the underground lifts and stairs. The woman is on the ground now, her Gucci handbag spilling its guts next to the front wheel of her BMW. You're kneeling beside her. Your left hand's clamped over her mouth, her throat. She barely struggles any more. Just some weak attempts at biting. There's a patch of motor oil near her outflung palm. Brighter colour is seeping from her clothing. Her eyes are looking up at you. Please, please,

please, *they say,* Don't kill me. You're a woman. We're women. Women don't kill women. *Her pupils are so black they appear white. An almost solemn moment. You tighten your grip over her mouth. Raise the knife. She flinches, jerks her head, rolls her eyes like a frightened horse. The pupils have grown so large there's nothing but whiteness now.*

That's when the knife plunges back in. 'Stupid bitch! There are women and *women!' Flecks of spittle have landed on her upturned face.* 'Equality! Solidarity! What crap!'

Pain ripped across her cheek. Laura's hand flew up. Bandit! She must have clutched him too tight and he'd fought back with his claws.

He'd got away unharmed, of course, up the bookshelf and on to the wardrobe. His eyes were burning sulphur in the blackness of his fur.

'Sorry. Sorry.' She reached out to him tentatively, but he only slunk away further, right up to the wall. 'Here, sweetheart.' She rattled the box with the salmon-flavoured biscuits, his favourites. He pretended not to hear, never even twitched his nose. She tried to miaow at him, again and again. He remained stubbornly silent.

Nothing worked today. Nothing. Not the running, not the library books, not the music. *That* least of all, it seemed. Not even the TV. So tense she was. Could be the heat. Or seeing the mirage woman in the yard. Or too much bloody food. All that meat they'd served for supper earlier – a woodcutter's steak, for God's sake! She was sure they used special E-numbers in the seasoning to make you overeat. She had fed a mouthful to Bandit, once he'd recovered from his sulking fit, and flushed the rest down the toilet.

Perhaps if she wrote to Coco, the journalist? Her most recent letter had arrived a couple of days ago, just after they'd met for the first time, and she'd not yet bothered to answer it. Journalists were the worst, she'd found. Nosy. Always grubbing in the dirt.

But Coco seemed all right. So far. She'd given her the apricots – with a clump of dope inside the most luscious-looking one. 'To help you sleep,' a tiny note said. The nightmare vision of the two ghost women with their rasping questions and the *drip-drip-drip* of their blood must have haunted Coco, too.

After a drink of tap water liberally sprinkled with dope, Laura felt calmer. She'd write to her parents, she decided. Her confession and the subsequent prison sentence had shocked them into a state of near-senile debility. On their last visit, a month ago, they'd been holding hands, their interlinked fingers scrabbling shakily against the security glass. They'd smiled and smiled; asked was she treated all right, did she get enough exercise and proper meals? Still, they'd always stuck by her. That was something, wasn't it? They'd rejected fifty grand from the biggest-selling Sunday tabloid for their side of the story.

But there is no story, goddammit. Except that you should have been allowed to join the police force. Instead, you'd ended up dating a detective. Which meant you heard all about the investigation as soon as they discovered the second body. (Stupid bitch couldn't expect anything less, could she, walking alone by the river at night?) A few weeks later you got Roland to discuss the leads they had on the spate of fires in your home town. The napkins were no news to you, of course. Nor the large-print messages on them in red ballpoint pen: I AM AN ARSONIST. WATCH OUT. THERE'LL BE A BIG BLAZE IN X TONIGHT. You for your part made Roland laugh by describing how you'd go about setting an office block on fire. Or a public toilet:

When the outer door closes, you listen to the retreating steps for a moment, then start to dismantle the toilet roll holder. You rip out the roll, loosen it into a flabby nest of paper, scatter some lighter fluid on top. A quick glance outside the cubicle – no-one around – and you strike seven matches (it would have to be seven, wouldn't it, for luck?). You drop them and run. There's no CCTV here, you checked that out beforehand. (In reality you always used a candle to ignite the fluid, to make it more of a ritual.)

Roland had never suspected a thing – he was in love with you, poor soul.

Laura slid the sheet of pale green paper under her pillow, for destruction later. As she lay there stroking and nuzzling Bandit in the dark, lavishing kisses on him, the words she'd written to her parents seemed to come smouldering through the pillowslip and the polyester filling:

Wasn't I a nice little girl? You tell me. Wasn't I normal? Even my misdemeanours as a teenager were normal, weren't they? But our life was such a bore. Our street was boring. Our town. The school. My various apprenticeships. A terrible stuffiness that bloated me until my skin grew thin and tight as a drum. I could hardly bend my legs any more or swing my arms, turn my head. I couldn't concentrate. Changing jobs every few months was merely a symptom. Going to the gym helped. My skin felt a little looser, but the dullness inside remained.

Eventually I forced myself to walk about town. I walked and walked. Mostly at night. Flexing my biceps, skipping, and pulling ferocious faces no-one could see.

The stalking started quite by chance. The rain came bucketing down that evening and the streets were deserted. Then suddenly a woman cut from a doorway right in front of me, her hood up, no umbrella. She never looked round. I was about to stride past when I slipped on something and half-knocked into her. She shied away with a choked cry, then bolted.

That was the trigger. I began to follow lone women. Gauged the level of their fear from the way they stiffened their necks, pressed their precious handbags to their breasts and quickened their step. I made them jump like startled deer. I craved their fear. And despised it. For a while I felt good and my skin sat more easily on me. But I needed to keep seeing their fear. Over and over and over.

Next morning Laura was in the wire cage again, exercising like a rat in the wheel. She'd been sick the previous night, after eating the sheet of pale green writing paper, torn into neat, palatable strips and helped down with several gulps of water. Maybe she was allergic to the ink, the chlorine, the dye. Or the words themselves. She'd spent half the night washing the pillowslip, then scrubbing the floor next to the bed, then the whole cell because by that time she was wide awake. When she tried giving Bandit a spot of grooming, though, he'd hissed at her and escaped under the bed.

Only 2.83 kilometres and already the heat was becoming oppressive; the air around her seemed charged with electricity. If she didn't want to die of sunstroke, she'd have to stop soon. Not that she gave a damn about her life; she knew she could never trust herself Outside again. But Bandit, what would happen to him without her?

'Loony Laura, Laura Loony, Loony Laura,' a voice suddenly squeaked behind her.

Laura yanked her head round. She couldn't see anyone. Was she going insane? Had the two ghosts started persecuting her during the day now as well?

A screechy giggle, and there was the mirage woman peeping round the beech tree: thin and old and unsavoury, with long, straggly grey hair and a scar that ran from below one eye right across the beaky nose and the other cheek. Unquestionably real. Laura's heart tightened. Surely, it couldn't be? Why would SHE be here?

Stamp-stamp-stamp went her feet, a fraction slower now.

'Frau Schuster?' she heard herself pant as she stared at the scar, fascinated.

The 'Loony Lauras' got louder.

The woman sounded crazy. And crazies couldn't testify in court, could they?

'Madeleine?'

Abrupt silence. Then the head nudged further round the tree trunk, exposing a chicken-skin throat with another scar that

11

started just below the left jaw and snaked down into the collar of the blouse. The eyes had narrowed and assumed their old pus-yellow; the nose seemed to hack at the tree bark.

'Madeleine?'

The eyes blinked rapidly – open and shut, open and shut. They had no lashes, and their corners were gritty with sleep. All at once, the woman raised her arm and, bony thumb and forefinger shaped into pincers, began plucking first at her naked lids, then the scraggly eyebrows.

Laura was getting angry now. *What the fuck's she playing at? Should be glad she's still alive, stupid old…* Suddenly she noticed how lopsided her running had become. Her right hand was up in the air, brandishing something invisible. Over by the bench ten metres away, Big Martha shifted from one foot to the other, gazing blankly. Laura forced a smile, forced her hand down by degrees, forced her fingers to curl round the rail once more. *Stay on an even keel, girl, an even keel.*

'Loony Laura, Laura Loony!' the squeaky voice resumed.

For a few seconds Laura managed to focus on her feet pushing away from the treadmill, but the continuous movement made her dizzy. When she glanced up, the old woman was standing in plain view in front of the tree and, tongue lolling, jabbing her fists towards the wire cage. The well-cut beige skirt and cream blouse hung on her body. She looked emaciated, like someone from a famine relief camp.

Laura couldn't help laughing, despite the fear she felt coiled inside.

'So that's where you've got to, dear.' A warden had appeared and was tugging at the old woman's sleeve to pull her away, out of range. 'The people here – they're dangerous, some of them. Very dangerous.'

As the day progressed, Laura's tension rose. She tried to convince herself that Frau Schuster had lost her mind and couldn't possibly have recognised her. Her own first name was an open secret, after all. It was pure coincidence, really, that the old woman had strayed near the wire cage. And yet ... she couldn't be a hundred percent sure.

The missing one percent is all that matters. It unbalances you. Maybe they sent her here on purpose. To torment you. Because no doubt they know who SHE is. Full of venom and jealousy until that final showdown. You'd left at once, with half a month's pay still owed you.

The so-called 'lake-front assault' was an accident, a complete accident. Seven at night, a gathering of pink-purple cottonwool clouds in the western sky. A balmy summer's evening. You'd no idea it was HER sitting on that bench by the water's edge. No idea. You'd been jogging along the path quite peacefully when, for no reason at all, she started screaming. For no reason at all, the stupid, stupid woman.

What pleasure to see the terror in those yellow eyes, like a sting going in, again and again. She couldn't have recognised you; you'd had your hair cut off by then and given up on the heavy make-up. And it was over in seconds, anyway. There she lay, face up so you were able to watch her fear to the last, half in, half out of the shallows, the red of the sky mirrored perfectly in the reddening swirls of the water.

Back home you chucked the knife into the rubbish and next morning the bin men got rid of it. Simple. No weapon ever found.

Then you heard the impossible: the woman was still alive.

But you've never been charged with that attack. And you've never confessed. It's your one secret. The gap at the foot of your bed, between the two ghosts. No need confessing to a botched job. A failure, to be honest. A failure.

Cradling Bandit in her lap, stroking and kissing him, Laura murmured, 'A failure, a failure, a failure.' He only yawned, arched his back and stiffened his legs. She lifted him up to her face. Nuzzled him. 'Come on, boy, give me a kiss. A kiss. Please.' As he turned his head away, his whiskers scratched her lips. 'Please?' The tip of his tail flicked up and down, against her arm. His paws had spread a little apart and the claws showed, bone white. Laura let go of him. 'Silly boy!' Her laughter didn't sound quite as hearty as she would have liked. So, on with the TV for a little distraction. MTV.

The video clip was one of those surreal numbers using computer-generated imagery. Vampire bats homing in on a blonde singer. Wings and webbed feet getting tangled in her hair. Gleaming incisors tearing at her lacy black top, grazing the tattoo on her throat. Then the music took off. Screeched and shrieked into the universe, shredded by multiple echo effects.

Bandit rushed up the bookshelf.

Now the music's got inside you. It's filling you, cramming itself into you until you begin to gag. Your skin's grown so tight you're about to explode. You leap to your feet, seize the cat, ripping him bodily from his retreat on the wardrobe, and start dancing.

The girl's face in the video changes every few seconds; first she's young and honey-skinned, golden-haired, then young and black, with dreadlocks and big, swelling breasts, pierced nipples, then older, greyer, bonier, her looks decaying, messed up by age and modern technology, the lips getting bloodless and thin, the fingers arthritic, the nose more and more hooked, the eyes glaring until they go yellow and scream at the screen. Scream at you, poison-bright.

'NO!' You fling yourself down on the bed with Bandit. When he tries to scramble away, you put him under the pillow for safety. When he tries to wriggle from underneath, you hold it down. For safety. But reflected on the pillow you can still see that face. Madeleine Schuster's face. Leering and stupid. Accusing.

You sit on the pillow. Hold it down on either side. Press your body down on it. Down, down, down. To erase what's there.

The Judas window clangs open.

'Laura, what the hell's going on? You're unsettling the others! Calm down or else –'

Down, down, down or else…

Muffled shouts along the corridor. Radios and TVs at full volume.

'And where's Bandit? Hiding up on the wardrobe again, is he? Poor Bandit. Just think of him, Laura. Think of how much you love him.'

Fists and feet hammering and kicking against doors. Heads hitting themselves against walls, over and over. And over.

'Bandit? Where are you? My love, where are you?'

Cool Room 3

Max Gruber first heard of the London bombings from his head gardener, who burst into the potting shed where he was putting together a batch of seedlings for the graves in the eastern corner of Oberkirch cemetery. The news had shocked him, of course – but living in Switzerland and working with the dead on a daily basis, he didn't feel particularly affected, or threatened. Not personally.

Except that next afternoon, when driving out of his private underground garage, he was suddenly blinded by the explosion of summer sunshine and let go of the steering wheel, raising his hands. Moments later his wife Rita hissed something he couldn't quite make out, as usual. Then life flicked back to normal. He'd only been trying to shield his eyes, hadn't he?

His son and daughter stood waiting in the shade of the gingko tree up the ramp, rucksacks at their feet, sticky ice cream cornets in even stickier fingers. Max stopped the Mercedes-Benz with a screech.

'Dammit!' he exclaimed as they slid into the polished leather seats, 'Who gave you these?' Neither of them bothered to reply and he glared at Rita for a second, then put on his sunglasses to hide the watery hurt in his eyes. And just so their ice cream wouldn't go into total meltdown, he set the air-conditioning at maximum. Rita hugged herself with both arms, ostentatiously. He stamped on the accelerator. The car lurched forward, still in gear.

The woman was a lost cause, Max knew. In the years following the birth of the two children his first wife hadn't been able to produce, Rita had gradually shed her outer layers of youthful brightness and warmth, like a poppy letting go of its petals, and had hardened into something else, something unyielding – a hoarder of terrible seeds. Her skull had begun to show through her skin, constantly reminding him of the bodies in the chapel of

16

rest; her lips had become bloodless and thin, and the morning-glory blue of her eyes that had first attracted him to her now resembled the tempered grey of his gardener's tools. Her teeth alone seemed to have grown more beautiful, brilliant white and gleaming, arranged in perfect rows like tiny gravestones, while she'd whisper in that velvety voice of hers which only the highest setting on his hearing aid could capture: 'You're an asshole, Max. If you don't get your act together, I'll leave you and take the kids.'

Why couldn't at least Peter, his son and eldest, respect his wishes? He didn't ask for much, did he? No ice cream or chocolate, he'd told them, not in *this* car. Peter was nearly fourteen, for pity's sake, yet he aped his mother, talking back at him or, even worse, ignoring him. Today, wearing those knee-hugging jeans, he looked like he was still in potty-training.

'Mm, that was delicious!' His daughter Anna licked her fingers with the exaggerated smacks of a five-year-old, although she was more than double that. Max tossed her the pack of wet wipes he kept in the glove compartment for emergencies, and she whined: 'I hate these, Dad. They smell like toilet cleaner.'

Rita reached for the bottle of Henniez mineral water in the holder and, turning in her seat so he couldn't see her face, handed it to Anna. Then they both laughed. Peter didn't – his eyes closed, shutting out the world around him, he was wired up to his iPod again. For once, Max was glad.

They were all ganging up against him. And here he was, chauffeuring them to their weekend chalet in the Toggenburg instead of looking after the cemetery garden-centre for another few hours. Late Friday afternoons were worth staying open for, especially at this time of year, just before the summer holidays, when folk wanted to make sure their loved ones would be adequately bedecked while they themselves got ready to bare their all on some exotic beach. Well, his own loved ones were alive and kicking and for the next couple of days would be soaking up the Alpine sun, overdosing on Coca Cola and half-melted slices of *sachertorte* from Meyer's, the local *confiserie*, as they lay splayed out amidst a clutter of magazines, mobiles, DVD players, iPods and computer games, like hawkers in some futuristic flea market.

Maybe his problem really was age – at sixty-five he was probably too old to be a father. That's certainly what Rita believed, calling him 'a bloody geriatric' whenever she thought his hearing aid was switched off. Or maybe his brain was going mushy – just like his gut, which was expanding by the day and beginning to hamper his work among the graves.

Max squared his jaws and indicated to join the *autobahn*. The Mercedes-Benz was his pride and joy, done out in burgundy calfskin, with a rosewood-and-leather dashboard, an in-built audio system that boasted eight speakers, and speed-proportional power steering. Driving it felt calming, almost like tending to the flower decorations in the chapel of rest.

He nodded to himself as he pictured the latest arrival there, in Cool Room 3, a silver-haired lady with soft, peaceful features, whose relatives had ordered several bouquets of roses, lilies and irises, and a posy of marigolds for her chest. The lady looked so much like his own mother, dead now for ten years, that he'd felt compelled to add a gift of his own, a small pot of gentians – his mother's favourites.

Max blinked. He was changing gears when something slithery-warm hit his hand.

'Oh,' Anna retched. 'Oh, oh.'

'Max!'

He swerved to an abrupt halt on the hard shoulder, too angry for words.

Rita rushed to help Anna from the car, then clasped the girl round her waist as she threw up in long, shuddering spurts into the weeds by the safety fence. Max turned away and reached for the wipes and paper hankies. Most of the vomit had landed between the front seats, on the centre armrest, the handbrake casing and in the folds around the gear stick.

'Forgot to take her travel-sickness tablets again, I bet,' Peter

18

commented from behind and with a 'Ugh, what a stink!' climbed out, plugged his earphones back in and waddle-walked over to the verge, the seat of his trousers midway down his legs.

Maybe the time had come to teach them all a lesson.

For a moment Max remained completely still. Then he pulled shut the passenger doors. Opened his own. Grabbed Rita's handbag, dumped it on the asphalt. Grabbed the rucksacks, dumped them, too. And flung out the soiled tissues in a final act of defiance. When he started up the engine, only Rita glanced round, assuming no doubt he wanted to keep the air conditioning running to reduce the smell.

In the rear view mirror he saw Peter struggling to catch up with the car, saw his mouth open and close in unheard shouts, saw him flail his hands – and give him the finger.

'And you,' Max said, quite unperturbed.

Shortly afterwards his mobile went. He let it ring for a while, then switched it off. Even a 'bloody geriatric' could pull off a stunt on occasion. 'Stuntman Max,' he muttered in his best American accent, grinning to himself. 'Stuntman Max.'

On the radio he found some New Orleans jazz and hummed along to it, upping the volume until his whole body seemed to vibrate. He hadn't felt so pleased with himself in years. Tapping the steering wheel in time, he decided to take the next exit and drive straight back home. He could do some more work in the nursery – the roses needed spraying again – or he could help Michael, his head gardener, to finish the replanting job in the cemetery's eastern corner. And if he didn't want to get his hands dirty, he could always re-open the flower shop for a couple of hours. Or – his fingers stopped drumming and he drew in his breath sharply – he could go up to the chapel of rest, unlock its doors, and visit Cool Room 3 with the old lady. Paying his respects, as it were.

The more his second marriage was falling apart, the more he missed his mother. Rita had become distant towards him, distant and spiteful, her initial playfulness replaced by a pent-up rage so intense it seemed to him that one day soon the force of it would crack her skull apart, letting her anger come spilling out like the black seeds from a poppy head.

But he would fight her – he'd never agree to her taking the kids away from him. Never!

He speeded up. He enjoyed driving fast for a change, weaving in and out of the lanes – a bit like slaloming down a mountainside. Rita would have complained, of course.

Who the hell did she think she was, anyway? The youngest of a houseful of starving immigrant kids, a lowly chef by training! And she knew she'd never been a looker, so why pretend otherwise? In the old days, when he and Rita still had dinner guests, he used to joke that men got married for all sorts of reasons, for beauty, money, children or good cooking, and that he, not being greedy, had restricted himself to only two of them. This usually earned him a few laughs, even from Rita. His most risqué jest, about the advantages of having an ugly wife, he'd reserved for special company, once he'd offered round the cigars and poured the Courvoisier.

Damn, he'd just missed the exit; his hearing may be going, but he'd better not lose his grip on reality. Not that his sense of smell seemed to be affected, unfortunately. Max wrinkled his nose at the lingering whiff of sick, and suddenly became aware of how hot he was feeling – as if he was having an attack of those menopausal flushes women were supposed to suffer from. He had a sip of the Henniez. It tasted tepid. Then he noticed that the flow of cool air had ceased and there was a little light on next to the AC symbol on the dashboard. A malfunction. He'd have to swap the Mercedes for a courtesy car at his dealership. With a sigh he zapped open the windows and sunroof. The whooshes of sultry summer air ripped the jazz into gasping shrieks of saxophone and trumpet until, sighing again, he tuned in to some talk-show station where voices rose and fell in soothing waves.

A new exit was approaching. When Max slowed down, the heat began to press in on him once more, pawing him like a child's sticky hands. He zapped the sunroof and windows shut. Abruptly the waves of voices separated into individual words and phrases, in English and German, their meaning anything but soothing:

'…was too loud for our ears to hear even. For a while there was nothing. Blackness. No sound. Then the screaming started. Smoke everywhere. People coughed and moaned. Cried. I found myself stumbling along the rails, blindly, away from the horror of it all…'

Max was about to switch back to music when an elderly man said, 'The worst of it is that we never had the chance to say goodbye. Never had the chance to make amends. Never had the chance…' The speaker began to sob, in between sobs repeating brokenly, 'We never … had the chance, never had … the chance, never –' before he was cut off by a mournful piece of classical music.

All of a sudden, travelling in the opposite direction now on the *autobahn*, Max heard what could only be his own voice reverberating inside his head, accusing him: 'What if something's happened to Rita and the kids?' As he listened, more and more stricken, he pictured terrifying scenarios: abductions at knife point, drunk drivers, drugged drivers, maniac drivers, crashes involving lorries, tankers. Until he almost burst into tears. And realised with a jolt that he was feeling sorry for himself – not for them. That he'd been hoping something *had* happened to his family in order to reproach himself, making a feast of his own failings. Adding spice to his empty existence. And wasn't that what he was going to do anyway, by returning to the old lady in Cool Room 3? Wasn't he trying to salvage something long dead and gone? Glorifying it? His mother had died ten years ago. Why the hell couldn't he live with the living? Even if he hated them – why couldn't he at least accept them?

He was beginning to feel hot again; the sweat was pouring off him. He had another drink of mineral water. Christ, was he going mad? He'd never believed in this kind of psycho-babble.

All that soul-searching stuff was for the crazies. He'd always been the proactive type, a man of action who did what he did, and knew what he did was right. Passing the spot where he had abandoned Rita and the kids, he strained to see them, but his view was blocked by several lorries engaged in one of their lethal chase games.

He knew he would take the next exit. Knew he would go back to pick them up. He would apologise. Grovel if necessary, though not too much.

The balls of tissue paper were still there, blown across the two lanes of the *autobahn* like the start and finish of a trail, the nightmare version of 'Hänsel and Gretel'.

Max drew up on the hard shoulder, stepped into the sweltering heat and went over to the safety fence, as if to check Rita hadn't used a wire-cutter to escape down the embankment with the kids.

So they had climbed into someone else's car. Had trusted a stranger. A stranger, for God's sake! Max began to roar. He roared along with the traffic noise. Roared until he could feel his head going purple, ready to burst – when, out of the corner of his eye, he glimpsed a flash of brightest crimson: wild poppies, a whole cluster of them. Their flimsy petals were fluttering and waving in the continuous air stream. Beckoning. He approached cautiously, as though they might explode and spit their black seeds at him. Then he pounced. And yanked out every single one of them.

After getting back into the car he drove more slowly, his shirt limp with sweat and clinging to his belly, the bunch of poppies on the passenger seat starting to look ragged, the mountains rearing up larger than life. Every so often, he took a swig of Henniez.

Even before he rounded the last hairpin bend, towards early evening, Max could tell there was no-one at the chalet. The outside shutters were closed, the garden chairs stacked and sheathed on the long balcony, the window boxes of geraniums laid out on the picnic table like a dusky pink and white table-cloth awaiting the neighbour's watering can. Everything had that feeling of suspended animation, that quivering, holding-one's-breath stillness he always sensed on opening the door after a week's absence.

He pulled into the neatly paved drive. He could have saved himself the trip, goddammit! Could have saved himself the anguish. Rita and the kids must have hitched a lift back home. By now they'd be all stoked up, spoiling for a fight, wondering where the hell he was. He seized the poppies next to him and began to tear off their petals, dropping them out of the car window by the fistful. When he had finished, he stuck the stalks with their skull heads into the empty Henniez bottle, like trophies. He U-turned and drove off without a backward glance, down the hairpin bends, through the Toggenburg roadside villages, back along the *autobahn*.

He reached Oberkirch just after nightfall.

Coasting towards his house, Max noticed there were no lights on, despite the darkness. What the hell were they playing at? They were sure to be home. Where else would they be? But already, in the pit of his stomach, he could feel the stone-heavy weight of dread. And as he drove past the gingko tree, down the ramp into the underground garage, he suddenly understood the elderly man on the radio, sobbing so hard – and he felt blinded now not by an explosion of summer sunshine but by a never-ending, tunnelling blackness.

Russian Blue

The day I got away from the White Coats behind the mountains I laughed for the first time in months. A laugh that seemed to stall and stutter until my whole being was bursting with it and there was no space left for the memory of Cupid-bow smiles and casual arm-locks, the chemical cocktails and bland food, no space left any more for that puke-pastel building flanked by cypresses like guards on permanent duty.

By then, of course, I had long crossed the river flowing past it all so demurely, in its straitjacket of concrete, and was well on my way.

They'd said I needed help, lots of help. Bribe a doctor, two doctors, some specialist and, hey bingo, she's all yours! But I was never theirs, whatever they might have thought. And they didn't help me either – I helped myself. Did what they wanted until I was allowed art therapy (with access to scissors, paints, fabrics, adhesives) to 'express myself'. That same night, I hacked my hair down to a stubble, wrapped a bandage round my chest and dressed in a set of men's clothes from the recycling bin. A dab of paint, some glue and jute, and I became Bernhard Neumann, slightly down-at-heel, swarthy, moustachioed, with a voice that seemed to growl and the sad brown eyes of a St Bernard.

They must have reported me missing the moment my room was found empty next morning. Posters, dusty by now and bleached by the summer heat, would have been tacked to the walls of police and railway stations, libraries, dosshouses, to telegraph poles and the trunks of the weeping willows in my home town. Below the picture of a frumpy, middle-aged woman called Clara Kummer, a 'greatly worried' husband would have been mentioned, though not the fact that he never once bothered to visit her in all the time the White Coats kept her locked up.

With barely two hundred francs saved from my 'personal luxuries' allowance, I made it to the Alps by the end of August, walking, hitching, picking fruit or vegetables in return for a hot meal and a bed, even begging on occasion. A generous farmer on Lake Constance had let me have his old pup tent and rucksack (with a Swiss Army Knife inside), and I'd got hold of a baseball cap and a pair of horn-rimmed glasses at a flea market. No-one would have recognised in Bernhard Neumann the good little wife-cum-cookery-teacher who'd always given outdoor activities a wide berth.

It was after a misty-golden trek along the lakes of the Upper Engadine and down the vertiginous drop of Maloja Pass into Val Bregaglia that I came across the Russian Blue.

Near the Italian border I'd climbed a steep mountain track past terraces of chestnut trees and tiny orchards of wasp-riddled fruit, unpruned vines and benches furred with moss and orange lichen towards a small settlement of houses. Even from a distance I could see the gaping holes in the roofs, black spaces in the mosaic of grey, ochre and silver-green granite tiles where birds flew in and out freely. The wooden verandas and balconies sagged as if under the combined weight of generations. The houses had been abandoned years ago.

Looking for a place to spend the night, I had just squeezed through a cellar door stuck permanently half-open when there was a miaow from the shadowy depths. Seconds later I felt something rub against my legs. The cat was beautiful, almost luminous in the semi-darkness, thin yet elegant like one of those Egyptian goddesses – and a bit like a ghost, too, with its bluish quicksilver coat, eerily prominent whisker pads and vivid green eyes: a ghost cat in a ghost house in a village full of ghost houses.

I backed away and the creature disappeared without a sound; for a moment I wondered if I'd merely imagined it, giving physical existence to a passing thought. I blame the White Coats for these flashes of unease, messing me up with their drugs.

But then, pushing my way out into the wind that had begun to smell of rain, I heard the miaow again, sharp this time and much louder, terminating in a heart-rending whimper – almost human-sounding. Despite my fear and an inner voice urging me to get the hell out, I couldn't resist following what was by now no more than an echo in my ears. I kept slipping on the damp cellar cobbles, stepped on debris that scrunched unnervingly under my feet, stepped into soft, wet, squishy things I preferred to think were old newspapers soaked to a pulp by decades of neglect. Then I reached another door, solid and slightly ajar. I inched it open with my walking stick.

No grisly secrets; the room was filled with firewood in straggly piles. Yet, for an instant, the scaly, discoloured branches reminded me of snakes poised to strike and I felt my insides go liquid with fear. The light had a sluggish, muddy quality, as if tainted by the only window, narrow, high up and thick with grime and cobwebs.

A sudden movement to my left made me recoil. The cat had emerged from round a heap of logs stacked into a low wall, its silver-blue coat near-electric. Its tail was up and the large ears seemed even more pointed as it stared at me, solemn and unblinking. After a while it arched its graceful neck and started rubbing against my legs, purring. I bent down to stroke it. Just then, there was a noise behind the logs.

I raised my stick. 'Who's there?' My voice was a squeak of tangled vocal cords.

No-one answered. The cat had darted away again, and all I could hear were the usual creakings, drippings and barely audible moanings, the bodily functions of most derelict buildings – before a volley of raindrops hit the windowpane like shrapnel.

I gripped my stick harder. 'Come on! Show yourself!'

Still no reply.

The cat gave another of its peremptory miaows and returned. It stopped a little in front of me, then took a couple of steps towards the stack of logs ... stopped and looked back at me ... took a few more steps ... stopped ... looked. Finally I followed.

The first thing I noticed were the brightly coloured women's clothes scattered around a large sports bag: a gentian-blue cardigan, a green silk blouse, a purple dress and matching underwear. An earthenware jug stood in a wet patch by the wall, next to a single purple stiletto and a carrier bag spilling chocolate wrappers, empty tins and crisp packets. I was about to crouch down for a better look when the cat miaowed again. It was sitting motionless behind another, smaller stack of logs, gazing at me. I smiled: of course, it wanted to show me its litter!

I approached cautiously – approached a wadded-up blanket on top of a sheet of plastic and some newspapers...

No, it was impossible! I turned away. How cruel the human mind can be, clawing at the very centre of one's heart, tearing it apart. I took several slow, deep breaths, then glanced over once more. But the baby was still there, tucked inside the blanket.

I dropped to my knees, put down my walking stick. The baby's eyes were closed. Saliva had dried on its chin. The lips were slack and waxy pale. As I looked into the tiny face, it seemed to dissolve into a translucency of skin, hair and bone. My fingers left silvery trails on the baby's cheeks. So cold they felt, as cold and implacable as the mountains standing guard behind the house.

All of a sudden the little mouth quivered. I snatched my hand away. The cat flicked the tip of its tail, stared at me with blade-thin pupils and lay down beside the baby, one front paw curled protectively across the blanket. As it did so, a flat round piece of wood the size of a pocket mirror slid from the fabric folds.

I picked it up. The icon was amateurish, kitschy even, but it cut me to the quick all the same. I felt as if I had violated a shrine, broken a spell or some kind of promise. How could I have forgotten about the baby's mother? She'd be nearby, had perhaps gone foraging for berries and sweet chestnuts and was now sheltering from the rain I could hear pelting down. But she wouldn't leave her child alone for long. No mother would. Though a few minutes could do it – ten minutes was enough, after all, one short trip to the baker's up the street for a loaf of bread – and the guilt would last a lifetime. In spite of what the White Coats said. They didn't understand, could never understand, not with all the training, textbooks and therapy in the world.

My scars had started to itch. I got to my feet, pulled back the sleeves of my leather jacket and those of my woollen jumper, then drew my wrists up and down the dirty wall, roughly, again and again, gritting my teeth until the pain made me gasp. Afterwards I hugged the wounds to myself like precious gifts. Bloodletting always helped to soothe me – and it still does, sometimes.

Before I left I kissed the baby and, on an impulse, grabbed the icon, telling myself I was in more need of it than *she* could ever be.

As I crossed the cellar's gloom towards the stuck-open door, I called out in my real voice, 'Hello? Is there anybody there? Hello? I don't mean you any harm, or your baby.' But I met no-one, not even outside, where the rain kept on falling, cold and unfeeling, more relentless than ever.

I chose a shed some thirty metres up the village lane, with a clear view of the cellar entrance, and settled down to wait, cushioned by my rucksack. I wanted to see the owner of that purple stiletto and the icon that was now in my pocket, wanted to find out why she had brought her baby to such a godforsaken place.

After a bit the rain eased off. The light began to fade and dusk came drifting down like smoke, softening the ruined aspect of the houses. I could feel the broken skin on my wrists tighten and pucker into new folds. I was healing too quickly.

I'd been waiting three quarters of an hour, getting worried sick about the baby, when I saw the ghost cat glide out the door. It hesitated a moment, lifted its head to sniff the air, then set off up the lane. A few minutes later it was back and again stood sniffing. As I watched, I heard an odd rustling sound and suddenly a bird of mythical proportions flapped past the shed – and just as suddenly transformed itself into a young woman, thin and scraggly-looking under a stiff plastic sheet with a slit for her head. She was carrying two rusty buckets. One of her trouser legs hung in tatters around her shin. She was limping badly.

I held my breath and watched. It felt good to be the hunter for once, not the hunted.

The plastic poncho scraped loudly against the door as the bird-woman went through the opening, followed by the Russian Blue. Then nothing. Then a scream, muffled at first. And then she came rushing out with the baby in its blanket, her face a pale disk that reflected the last of the light, her mouth and eyes vague smudges. Hair flying, plastic flapping, she half-limped, half-ran downhill, shrieking, stumbling, barely catching herself when she tried to glance back over her shoulder. She looked just like another maniac escapee from the puke-pastel building behind the mountains, ready for a calming shot from the White Coats. What the hell was she scared of? I'd only taken the icon; I hadn't hurt a hair on her child's head.

Then I remembered about the blood: my blood on the wall of the storeroom and maybe on the baby's cheeks, too.

'Hey, you! Stop! Don't be afraid!'

But she'd already vanished behind one of the ghost houses.

I gave chase – down the ghost lane of the ghost village, into the deepening twilight of a chestnut grove that seemed the only living, growing thing for miles around.

A few metres into the small wood the bird-woman tripped again, stumbled for the last time and pitched forward with a thud, only just managing to twist her body round to protect the baby from the fall. I heard her moan. At my approach she tried wildly to scramble away, clawing at a tree trunk like an animal and half-hauling herself up, spitting at me and shouting things in a guttural language, her voice raw with emotion – before she finally collapsed in a huddle of torn plastic. She lay sprawled and still, without a whimper, shielding the baby that had begun to mewl quietly, as if under its breath, shielding it from me – *me*, of all people! One of her legs was exposed and a bone stuck out from her shin like the splintered end of a skewer. It looked so crazily unreal I started to giggle. Then I gagged.

Next morning, a grey, drizzly, miserable sort of day, I was on a mountain track leading up towards the Maloja Pass again, feeling ragged and a little light-headed from lack of sleep. I had no idea how I'd got there. The rucksack dragged on my back. My glasses and cap were gone; my tongue kept wetting my lips, bare and vulnerable without the moustache; my breasts, released from their bandage, swung free under an unfamiliar black sweatshirt. I must have ditched my Neumann disguise during the night. The bird-woman, the baby and the cat with the luminous eyes were far away, just three more fragments of someone else's memory left to haunt the abandoned settlement.

Around midday I reached the ruins of an old Roman watch-tower in the woods somewhere below the summit and sat down for a rest. My lunch consisted of some hardened cheese and a few stale crackers from my rucksack. No more bread for me, ever, not since that trip to the baker's which cost me my child. No more Lord's Prayer either. No more White Coats with syringes, trying to convince me that bread has nothing to do with flesh, the dead flesh of an infant who'd managed to crawl to the bathroom and put her head inside a plastic shower cap...

I was gazing at the icon when I felt something flick against the back of my legs. I looked. Then leapt up, cursing the White Coats and their chemical cocktails. But the Russian Blue was still there – crouching at a safe distance now – its magic blue fur, exaggerated whisker pads and green almond eyes quite unmistakable. And even though I told myself that I had done nothing wrong, I felt another of those flashes of unease.

I tried to ignore the cat stalking me like a shadow, tried to ignore its plaintive, intermittent miaows and the soft stealth of its paws on the pine needles. In the end I jumped across a fast-flowing stream – cats hate water, simple as that. I sighed with relief.

Ten minutes later there was a rustle in the undergrowth. The green stare was almost human – reproachful, angry-hurt.

By mid-afternoon I'd had enough. Under cover of some trees near the village of Maloja, I trimmed my hair with the Swiss Army Knife, rolled a large handkerchief into a headband, lined my eyes with Bernhard Neumann's eyebrow pencil, pinched some colour into my cheeks and, hey presto, I'd turned into one of those fortyish women with a still-youthful glow to their skin, discreet makeup, hair cropped rakishly short under a pirate-style scarf, ready to cadge a lift from any passing motorist.

I was picked up by a local in a Range Rover who drove like the devil. The Russian Blue was left behind in a cloud of hellfire exhaust fumes – perhaps it had never existed, after all, except in those blurred reaches of my mind.

The driver had wiry grey hair and the leathery skin of a part-time farmer, part-time ski-lift operator. His brown eyes lacked definition, as if they'd been melted by the Alpine sun. He was smoking a pipe and had the radio on, a Romansch station. I was glad there was no need for small talk. Then the news came on. That's when the man started muttering to himself, his words slurred by the pipe between his lips. At first I didn't pay any attention. Until I realised he was talking in Swiss German, not Romansch.

'Good riddance,' he kept repeating, 'good riddance, yes.' All at once he slowed down, removed the pipe and cocked his head at me, 'What do you think?'

'Excuse me?' I smiled nervously, my fingers clenching the penknife in my pocket.

'Illegal immigrants, I said. We've got enough foreigners in this country already, haven't we? Buying up all our good land, agricultural land at that, for their goddamn holiday chalets. So who's to complain if one or two of them get rubbed out occasionally, eh?'

He speeded up again and I loosened my grip on the knife. But then, suddenly, I felt a cold wind blowing right through me, like I was a kite made of rice paper, glue and balsa wood, at the mercy of the weather and some invisible hand, far below.

'It's all for the better,' the man kept saying.

I nodded feebly, shaken by that icy gust out of nowhere, nameless and quite beyond my understanding.

A week later I was sitting in a restaurant in the Lower Engadine, reading the paper.

On the front page was the picture of the bird-woman, not dishevelled now but rather pretty, with high cheekbones and big eyes. Someone, apparently, had given the police an anonymous tip-off, saying there was an injured woman up in the mountains. When she was rescued, she'd reported a man with glasses and a moustache who had pursued her and tried to wrench the child from her arms. A phantom, the police maintained. A ruse to escape the murder charges they were bringing against her. Because, yes, they *had* found a man. A man without glasses or moustache – and he was dead. Cause of death: a brain haemorrhage after a severe blow to the head, probably from a rock. The woman had every reason to hate that man, it seemed. He'd trafficked her into Italy from Ukraine and exploited her as a prostitute for years.

Glancing out the open back door into the shadows of the restaurant garden, I took a sip of coffee and told myself that although she'd been put into prison, the bird-woman was at least safe. And her baby, too. Whatever had happened, they were both safe now. Just like me. I was proud of myself – I'd managed to leave the child behind and bury my hopes of ever being a mother.

I had another sip, then slid the newspaper up on the table to gaze at the icon concealed on my lap. Crude as it was, the love it expressed made my eyes water yet again and I touched a finger to the golden halo around the two figures, to draw strength. Feeling the faint ridge between the different layers of paint, I caught myself thinking, What if the bird-woman shouldn't be in prison at all? What if it should be *me*? Not that I had any recollection of committing a crime. Of attacking a man. Only a vague impression of someone unshaven, with a strong nose and full lips. Just like the victim's face in the grainy newspaper photo in front of me. And just like my husband had looked when I last dreamed of him, months and months ago.

One day, I promised myself as I finished my coffee, one day I would visit the bird-woman in prison. Maybe I would even return the icon to her.

From the restaurant garden came a sudden soft patter, more like an echo in my ears, then there was a flash of silvery blue, so fast I still can't be sure it was real.

The Death Queue

The first time your daughter phoned was three weeks ago, late morning. You'd once told me she didn't trust me, had never trusted any of your women friends, but not to worry: Claudia was grown up now, and your affairs were none of her business.

This was different. 'An emergency,' she said, and there were tears in her voice. 'They found him unconscious on the office floor; Diva wouldn't stop barking and whimpering. Now he's in intensive care.' She sniffed, blew her nose. 'Lung cancer. Inoperable. I thought you might…'

I didn't wait to hear the rest. Sharp-edged things knocked into me as I gasped my way towards the window. My mouth had torn open to suck in the air, all the air in the room, the flat, the building. My lungs filled with dank shreds of autumn fog as I hung over the windowsill in the oversized sweatshirt I wear now that I hardly leave the house any more. Whole convoys of lorries might have thundered past on the street below, flashing their lights, whole brigades of shoppers with staring eyes and clanging tins, jars and bottles, pavementfuls of shrill clattering schoolchildren – what the hell did I care.

Once I'd recovered myself and retrieved the phone from the floor, the line was dead. I decided to write to her instead. Dug out some notepaper from under a pile of glossy old theatre programmes and take-away menus in a drawer I still haven't had the energy to clear out so others won't have to, later.

19 October, noon, Flat 3, Zürcherstrasse 7A I put in my usual left-handed spider-sprawl, then paused. Fancy me, of all people, feeling the need to pinpoint my coordinates in time and space!

Dear Claudia – I paused again. I hate writing things, especially letters. And the girl's a virtual stranger, even if she *is* your daughter. The sleeve of my sweatshirt had smeared her name, but I couldn't bear starting over. She'd assume I'd been crying, which I suppose

34

I was, in a dry, inside sort of way. I continued, quickly now, to be done with it:

I'm terribly sorry about your father… Adrian has always seemed so fit and well, going for runs with Diva, playing squash, tennis, badminton. There was no sign of anything wrong with him the last time we met, in summer. And he never complained, never said a word about being in pain.

I stopped myself from adding: Surely, this is a mistake. Because it should have been me, not him. I'm the one that's ill, has been ill for years. Not him. I'm the one that's supposed to be dying, for God's sake!

In the end I scrawled, *You're in my thoughts, and so is Adrian. Poor dear Adrian…* And rushed off to the bathroom. My nose had started bleeding again. As I crouched and retched into the toilet bowl, I could feel the brittleness of my left jaw, my teeth rattling like gravel, so loose now, so frighteningly loose.

Then came her voicemail message on Tuesday night.

I'd been having one of my mammoth phone sessions: two and a half fluid hours of vodka (an excellent painkiller) and a chat with Jenny, at twenty-four one of my youngest friends. You were always amazed (or is 'envious' more to the point?) that most of my closest friends are half my age. Is *this* maybe the secret of eternal youth: not creams or peels or plastic surgery, but the sheer openness of allowing one's younger self to be alive and laugh and cry along with the young? Anyway, Jenny had been accused of 'carrying on' with a seventeen-year-old pupil from her French class ('A real hunk of jailbait, and no innocent,' she described him, leering audibly) and needed a bit of advice on how to straighten matters out with the school board.

Before listening to my messages, I got myself another refill on the rocks and collapsed into the chintzy sofa, one of the few relics salvaged from my first marriage. I was suddenly exhausted. My hands were shaking so much the slim strips of maroon polish down the middle of my nails seemed to writhe and multiply.

Christ, I used to be able to stay up till all hours, looking good, flirting and holding my drink, but this new round of chemo is getting to me – I seem to shrink overnight and wake up sad and bleeding, my mouth clogged with disgust. I swigged some vodka to rid myself of the taste that's with me now at all times, the taste of my own decay, then I punched the 'Play' button.

And there was her message, a wavering blur of sobs: 'It's Claudia here. Please call me.'

To be honest, I hesitated for a minute or two, drank down the entire glass to prepare myself for what I'd already guessed was coming.

Why not me? I couldn't help thinking. Why do others get to jump the death queue, and not me? Almost immediately, of course, I felt guilty. Ashamed of myself. The large papery fronds of my indoor palm tree rustled their reproach in the faint draught from the hall, and I shivered. It had been a windy afternoon, cold, with the occasional flurry of bright, gritty rain pinging off the windowpanes and dead leaves scraping and scuttling across the concrete of the balcony floor. The alcohol I'd consumed that evening, the only 'food' my stomach appears to accept without complaint these days, had made my eyes water. I wanted nothing more than to crawl into a corner of my sofa and hide myself there like a cat, for no-one to find and stroke back to life.

Claudia just cried for a while and I sat listening, crumpled into my corner, eyes closed, doing my best not to let go of the phone. When she finally managed to tell me that you'd died on Sunday without regaining consciousness, I felt genuinely happy for you. You'd have hated being dependent. Remember what you said that weekend in April? 'Let's agree on a buffer zone where we can meet without trespassing, without imposing or committing ourselves.' Pure legalese, and at first I'd screamed at you, I was so bloody furious. Remember how in answer you took my hands, quietly turned them over and, one by one, kissed the soft pads of my fingers? Something inside me flipped over then, and I smiled against my will. But there won't be any more buffer zones now. Only a place in my memory that will always be ours.

Claudia started sniffling again. 'The cremation is on Thursday. You're very welcome.'

I swallowed hard and stared over at the rustling palm fronds as if they could soothe away the sudden queasiness I felt.

'I don't think that would be a good idea, Claudia,' I said at last. 'I'll be paying my respects in private, here.'

Perhaps I imagined it, but her 'I understand' sounded relieved. She'll never trust me now, I know. Then she said, in an odd, flinty tone: 'I almost forgot, he left something for you' – and I realised she was jealous.

Can you picture it? Your healthy, young daughter jealous of me, a middle-aged woman with a tired, disintegrating body that's become a battlefield for surgeons? (The consolation is that the growths can't go much further now they've reached my head.)

For a moment I remained silent, wondered what on earth you could have possibly wanted me to have. My weight in gold, maybe? (I could do with that.)

'Father's associate will bring it round – Karl von Arp. He offered to, actually.'

I ignored her unspoken question. I could have told her, Yeah, you're right: Karl and I have always had a soft spot for each other, but nothing's ever happened. Because of your father. Satisfied? Brushing it all aside, I said, 'That's very nice of him. Any time is fine. As long as it's evenings.'

My feeble joke fell on stony ground, as expected, and we finished soon afterwards.

No-one appeared the following evening. Instead, Jürgen rang, the features editor of *Weltwoche* (and a former lover, why not admit it). He persuaded me to do some more proofreading for him, no doubt to bolster my sagging bank balance, and perhaps my self-esteem. 'Flexi-time,' he coaxed, 'plus you work from home. I'll drop off a laptop and get you onto the net, sweet as a kiss.' How could I refuse? And I was rather looking forward to seeing him.

I'd barely replenished my glass and buttered a slice of white bread, soft and crustless to minimise the pain of chewing, when the phone rang again: Floriano, my ex-brother-in-law. Regaling me with tales of his mother's senile dementia – that afternoon, she'd apparently mistaken his iPod for a hamster and insisted on feeding it. And so on and so on.

My third caller was Jane, minutes later.

'Oh,' she said, 'you're quick. So desperate you're waiting by the phone now? Only kidding!'

I laughed, sipped more drink.

Sad old Jane. Sharp as a broken needle. You'd met her twice, and didn't like her. 'Maladjusted' and 'neurotic' were some of your kinder remarks. I just feel sorry for her. Pale, beautiful Jane who went through primary school half-starved because her parents had a dozen kids and no money – until they were catapulted into riches-ville after her father won the lottery.

And now her newest husband has been diagnosed with prostate cancer.

'Perhaps he fucked around too much when he was young,' she blurted out. 'Least, that's what I heard on the radio recently: too many partners from too young.'

All at once I'd had it. Why do people always choose *me*, for Christ's sake? Turning me into some bloody confessor figure, asking me for absolution of what – their own callousness? 'Sorry, Jane,' I almost shouted, 'but that's not my problem. You want to discuss it, go and see his doctor. Ciao,' and, reaching down for the phone plug, I slipped it out of the socket, smooth as anything. I was surprised at myself, and pleased. Peace at last.

I kept the phone unplugged throughout Thursday. Even while I was out at the shops for a fresh bottle of vodka, some French Brie and tomatoes. Then at the doctor's to have my pharynx drained, a disgusting thrice-weekly necessity I'll never get used to, let alone be able to perform myself – not in this life, at any rate. All that stinking slime, that sludge... Do you remember how one night in a moment of grandiose passion – love conquers all, that kind of stuff – you'd vowed you would do it for me? And how, once acquainted with the finer details, you convincingly argued your way out of the job? You were never one for the grim physicalities of existence, were you, Adrian? As darkness fell and the wind picked up again, howling as if in agony, slapping my windows with wet, teary drops, I knew that you had passed through the fire, or the fire through you. And that you were truly gone.

Next evening Karl turned up with a plastic bag, a chilled bottle of Bollinger and a sad, forced smile that made the thick tendons in his throat strain like ropes. He was ten minutes early, but I was ready for him. Thank God I'd had the sense to reconnect the phone. There'd even been time for a quick bath and change, a mouthwash and several generous squirts of Opium.

I'd forgotten how burly he was (in Jenny-speak, definitely another 'real hunk') and must have gaped at him as he stood looking at me, his lavender eyes skimming over my black dress (my favourite because its cut gives the illusion of curves), then lingering on my face. On my hair – which is still my own. Still down to my shoulders, wheat blonde and frizzy. My one pride and joy, and a token of how much I've suffered. Worth the most paralysing arctic cold from that ice-blue chemo cap, worth the most punishing headaches.

'Your hair is beautiful,' he said eventually and, setting down the carrier bag and the champagne on the hall floor, he folded me in his arms as if I was breakable.

I pressed myself against him to prove I did have some strength left. I could feel his big body slump a little, then begin to tremble. For a long moment we held on to each other, clinging, trembling together, dancing our slow, swaying dance of loss.

'Poor you,' he whispered after a while, a little ambiguously, before adding, 'Adrian was such a good man. Any tricky case, and he'd be there to guide me through the legal maze.'

Rubbing my head on the shoulder of his soft wool jacket, I breathed in his smell: a mixture of cigarette smoke, faded after-shave, deodorant, and pure male muskiness – in the last few years I've become an expert at identifying bodily odours.

'You know,' he continued, 'what bothers me is that Adrian never once mentioned feeling unwell. Though the doctors believe he must have been in severe pain.' He lifted my chin carefully with one hand. 'Did he ever say anything to you?'

I shook my head, not quite trusting my voice, and closed my eyes so he wouldn't see … what? My confusion? My disappoint-ment at confidences unshared? Or self-pity, naked and ugly? I caught myself sneaking a glance at the plastic bag and speculating about your bequest.

After Karl had opened the Bollinger, easing out the cork with the softest of pops, we chinked glasses. 'Well, cheers!' he said, then suddenly checked himself. Started blinking: 'That's what he'd have wanted us to do, no?'

I nodded and wedged myself deeper into the corner of the sofa, legs tucked safely underneath (the idea of sitting with my feet dangling free, two inches off the floor, seemed too daunting). The black fabric of my dress lay creased around my knees, but I resisted the urge to pat it down and drank the champagne in quick, searing sips.

Karl had been watching me and now leant back in his arm-chair, his left hand brushing over his darkened eyes. He sounded husky when he spoke: 'I don't blame you for not going to the funeral yesterday…' Again his hand strayed near his eyes.

'Well, chances are I'll be at the next one.' I gave a short laugh and tossed my hair, trying to convince myself it's better to die with laughter lines than etchings of grief. Have a dance, come on, an inner voice prompted me – I wondered for a second whether that could have been you? Then I heard myself say it out loud: 'Let's dance,' and I flushed at my recklessness.

Without waiting for a reply I slid off the sofa and swished past the palm fronds, leaving them bobbing and fluttering like a group of flustered heads. Something sharp and rappy, I kept thinking, sharp and rappy, as I bent over the sound system squeezed between the CDs on my wall-to-wall brick-and-board bookshelf. My eyes flicked from Bach, Beethoven and Brahms to The Beatles, from Dvořák to Marlene Dietrich to Dire Straits. Karl's ominous silence unnerved me and I grabbed one, fumbled the disc into the machine and pressed 'Play'.

'Break On Through' boomed out of the speakers. My spine tingled at the eerie appropriateness of that song. *Weird Scenes Inside the Gold Mine* by The Doors, plucked from the shelf blindly, it seemed. Smiling, I swung round to Karl, in time to the beat. 'How about this for starters?'

But he sat frowning at me as if I'd gone crazy. After an endless pause he looked away, brought out a packet of Marlboros and, still frowning, started to tap one loose, then abruptly squashed it between his fingers, dropping the crumbly remains on the coffee table. 'Sorry,' he mouthed and poured himself more champagne. Gulped it in one. Coughed. And snatched up the plastic bag he'd placed beside his chair, as if in a hurry to get things over with, and get away.

'Please,' I said, 'not now. Later.' I went and took him by the hand, pulled. 'Please, Karl.'

At some point during 'Love Street' he mumbled into my ear that I was like a ballerina, just as delicate. That all he wanted was to put me in his pocket and carry me around with him, always. By then, of course, we'd had the Bollinger and were well into a bottle of Rioja.

I waited to open the bag until Karl had driven off. My nose felt swollen again and I hoped to God it wouldn't start bleeding. 'Three hours at most,' the doctor in Emergency had warned me, ten days ago. 'If it doesn't stop by itself within three hours, you have to come here.' There was no need for him to make his meaning plain, I could guess the 'or else'.

A box. A battered-looking, splotchy grey shoebox tied with

string and knotted. Men's Boots, a small label said at the side, size 11, black. On the lid was my name, printed in crimson, your handwriting unmistakable.

I cut the string with the kitchen scissors and found – not ashes, but letters. Yours to me: never-sent fragments of beginnings, of half-pages and pages, many of them marred by heavily scored-out words and phrases, most breaking off in mid-sentence, and each and every one unsigned, bearing witness to your lawyerly scruples.

Dearest, the most recent bit-page read (dated 12 August), I've vowed to finish and post this epistle, if only to prove to myself I can still manage my own affairs (!) without ~~recourse to~~ the help of a secretary. ~~Let me say how much I loved~~ I really enjoyed being with you last weekend. How ~~blissful~~ wonderful if we could spend a few days over New Year together. What do you ~~think~~ say? Karl has told me about a ~~nice~~ charming little hotel near the mountains where he stayed in spring. Very discreet and rather comfortable according to him (they offer breakfast in bed so you wouldn't have to get up). Or we could go ~~wherever you like~~ – And there your pen or your patience ran out. Odd you never actually talked to me about this. And now it will never happen.

The shoebox also contained a handful of letters I'd written to you, and I threw them out at once – they were yours.

Then came the photos. Photos I had no notion existed, of us both, snapped on the sly because, God knows (and you certainly did!) I'd have refused to pose for them. I glanced through the pile, feeling slightly sick, almost dizzy, despite another painkiller. The pictures had mainly been taken in restaurants (easy to slip a waiter a tip and the camera, yes?). The only one I've decided to keep is from some boat trip I can't even remember, with the wind whipping the hair around our faces.

The rest of the box seemed filled with decorations, menus and place settings from parties we'd been invited to: your name writing itself over and over again before my eyes until it was a blur of curves and straights and slashes, totally lost in the midst of glitter-wrapped sweets, tiny umbrellas from sundaes or long drinks, and ancient chocolate hearts.

Underneath it all were layers and layers of paper napkins. What a hoarder you were! At least, that's what I thought at first. But when I seized the topmost, several pressed flowers fell out – slightly faded yet recognisably gentians and edelweiss. The next one revealed two nearly black *rapunzel*-rampions and a Venus's slipper. I've now laid them out on my coffee table – all the flowers you ever gathered during our walks. Or rather your walks with and without Diva, while I relaxed in cafés and restaurants. The gentians were still a deep summer-sky blue...

I do remember that trip. Going up the mountains in a cable car and the slack lurch in the pit of my stomach, that split-second's free fall every time we passed a support pillar. And later the gourmet lunch at the hotel, then me in a deckchair on the sun-drenched terrace, a book and a half-bottle of wine for company while you went off hiking. How irritated you were to find me, on your return, in the very same place, laughing and squinting up at you in the brightness of the afternoon, the empty bottle raised in welcome.

Sitting here now, I toast my former self on that hotel terrace in the Alps and see my reflection stare back at me from the polished crystal of my glass of Rioja. The skin's stretched tight, the eyes are pools of darkness, the cheekbones curved to distortion, and everything's mottled by the rustling shadows of the palm fronds.

Two weeks. Two weeks was all it took you to die.

Slowly the reflection begins to disappear as I watch, and wait.

I Call Her Salome

A homage to Niki de Saint Phalle

The French ambassador's wife had a sip of rosé, paused briefly, then told me without any preamble, 'I don't think I've ever been moved by anything, or anyone, in my life.'

Her image remains with me even now: young, poised and cultured, yet with the sudden fragility of a much older woman, like a figure carved from crystal, ready to shatter to pieces in the blink of an eye – the way her glass did, seconds later.

It was this incident at the French Embassy in a small Middle East kingdom that was the beginning of everything, and the end: the end of a life-long evasion, the beginning of my makings as a true and widely acclaimed sculptor, the father of 'Salome'.

I admit I had egged Mme Durandard on, tried to get her to talk about the looming US military intervention in nearby Iraq, about her fears, her hopes and dreams, encouraging her to behave more like a flesh-and-blood person, not simply an official title – or a lifeless moquette.

Maybe it was mere clumsiness that made her knock over the wineglass. Maybe. Whatever the cause, the sound of breaking glass was enough to silence the conversation around the large dinner table and we all sat frozen – sheikhs, diplomats, businessmen, members and friends of Alliance Française. Sat and watched the crystal disk of the base, which had split clean off the stem, skitter-dance across the tabletop, preening itself in the mirror-sheen of the wood as it spun round and round in sharp glints of echo.

At the far end of the table the ambassador's shiny, well-bred face had turned an inauspicious shade of purple; his fingers around the dessert spoon were clenched into a fist. The dinner reception had been designed as a friendly, civilised gesture expressing France's continuing goodwill towards the Middle East, carefully orchestrated against a background of escalating

American threats and troop movements on the Kuwaiti/Iraqi border. Behind the ambassador on the windowsill, several pink and white orchids were balancing on their curving stems like birds about to take flight.

Mme Durandard had grown quite rigid. She reminded me of a puppet abandoned by her puppeteer – or an unfinished sculpture. For a moment I went into a daydream, found myself back in my grandmother's workshop with its piles of animal hides, imagined one of those skins stretched tight across a ribcage of wire-mesh ...

When I looked up again, the servants had cleared away the mess of shards and spilt wine, the ambassador had regained his ambassadorial composure and the room was once more filled with the hum of voices and the clink of dessert spoons.

Everything seemed exactly the same as before, except that Mme Durandard was no longer in her chair. But she had left something behind, something small and indispensable, half hidden by the crumpled napkin beside her untouched plate of vanilla crème brûlée and chocolate truffle. I slipped it into my pocket. Then excused myself to my neighbour, a French novelist with bright henna hair and even brighter jewellery. She inclined her head flirtatiously, letting her dangly earrings and the lucky charms on her necklace – every single key, heart and cockerel – wink at me. Why was it I always got seated next to some 'eligible' woman who could easily pass for my mother? I didn't need mothering now, not after all these years.

Stepping from the dining room, I pictured the old dog kennel at the bottom of my father's vast, overgrown garden near the woods and vineyards above Lake Geneva, outside Lausanne. It wasn't so much a kennel as a derelict shed enclosed by rust-eaten wire fencing that was mostly holes. I used to spend my nights there as a boy. For company I had Zara the Invisible, the strongest Alsatian I could conjure up for my protection. My mother's name had been Sara, though I wasn't supposed to remember because she'd gone off with another woman, just after my eighth birthday. My grandmother set up house with us instead, bringing with her heaps of sharply pungent animal hides to be cut up and made into bags, rucksacks, wallets, purses, belts. That's when I took to retreating to the shed. I'd lie there perfectly still and with my eyes closed … until I could smell Zara's warm, living dog smell, could hear her breathing, hear her muffled yelps or growls and the scuffling of her paws as she chased squirrels and rabbits in and out of the shadowy corners of her dreams. Sometimes, befuddled by sleep, I curled my fingers around nothing and felt I was holding one of her twitchy, trembling legs. Soothed by the flurries of cool, dark air that came through the chinks and knotholes in the walls and brought with them the scents of the seasons – fresh rain or snow, sappy leaves, dry earth and grapes full of sun heat, apples and plums rotting on the ground, rose petals blowing in the wind – I knew it was the saltiness of Zara's wet nose I tasted as I pretend-kissed her goodnight.

I smiled at the memory; I was grown up now, after all, and able to smile at anything, even if it hurt. Just then I caught a whiff of eau de Cologne from the liveried Filipino servant with the pencil moustache who was stationed in the entrance hall. I prolonged my smile. Near him, a wide staircase swung up towards an enormous, unlit chandelier that seemed to glow and flicker in the twilight as if phosphorescent. Perhaps it too had memories and was reflecting the ghosts of past things, past deeds, past lives.

There were only three people out on the terrace – a couple of diplomats and a sheikh from the Royal Family. They stood talking quietly by the stone balustrade, silhouetted against the luminous night sky in which the full moon hung suspended like a silver gong, and quite unaware of the wild cats prowling around the hibiscus trees and date palms. Mme Durandard had told me she fed the cats every evening and that some of them had become tame enough to trust her touch. But there was no sign of her now, or of the food bowls for her strays.

In the hall the servant gave me a cordial nod, then, realising I was making straight for the stairs, his expression changed.

'Private,' he said, and his moustache wriggled like a caterpillar. 'Sorry, sir. The bathroom is over here. Please.' He indicated an archway and took a step towards me.

'Don't worry, I'll be back in a sec!' I ran upstairs two at a time.

The doors on the first floor were all closed and, on a hunch, I climbed to the top.

Mme Durandard was huddled on a divan at the far end, next to a sago palm under an open skylight. In the silvery wash of the moon her face looked as still and bleached as a statue's. Only her mouth glistened faintly as if wounded, and her kohl-rimmed lids were dark and crude as dried blood.

I hesitated a moment – tried to commit her pose to memory and the way the light slanted down her face and shoulders, down the folds of her silk evening dress, over breasts, hips and drawn-up knees, down to her naked toes. Then, clearing my throat because she didn't seem to have either heard or seen me approach, I mumbled, 'I think you've lost something.' I reached into my pocket and placed the wedding ring on the small, glass-topped table beside her. She still didn't acknowledge me, or the ring.

I looked out at the moon – and made a wish.

Just then there were voices and an armed guard came striding towards me, followed by the Filipino servant, who panted anxiously, 'Mme Durandard … are you … okay?'

The guard halted only inches from me. 'Sorry, *monsieur*,' he growled in a nasty undertone, 'no access here. You leave now.' He leaned into my face and glared, hard. His breath smelt of seafood – he must have helped himself to the prawn cocktail leftovers in the kitchen. I was suppressing a grin when I noticed his hand. It was resting on his holster.

The ambassador's wife still hadn't uttered a word. Nor did she seem bothered about the gun. Instead, all at once, she half-rose from the divan, grabbed the ring and, with a piercing cry, flung it out into the night. A fleeting sparkle and it was gone, swallowed up by the darkness and, who knows, some funnel-shaped leaf or exotic flower that trapped things, or maybe it had simply got buried in the sandy soil which, so I'd been told on my arrival at the embassy, had long ago been reclaimed from the sea.

'It's your fault!' Mme Durandard screamed.

She was looking at me. Why me?

'Disgusting, prying little man. I hate you! Hate you! Hate you!'

I became just another ghostly reflection in the chandelier as I was being hauled downstairs by the guard. Meanwhile, the Filipino servant attempted in vain to calm the woman. She had started to sob now, loud, high, hiccoughy gasps that, from a distance, sounded more like shrieks of laughter.

I hoped she would come to her senses before the dinner party broke up, in time to send someone into the garden to search for her ring…

But I didn't wait around. I fled, guilty as charged – or rather, as I felt, guilty as judged. Fled like a coward because I couldn't bear the raw dislike, hatred even, I saw in the faces of the cook and the servants who had gathered at the bottom of the stairs. It was like in the souk, ever since the invasion of Afghanistan: the tailors would lift their feet off the treadles of their old-fashioned sewing machines and watch in silence as I chose a piece of clothing – a shirt, say, or a pair of Bedouin trousers whose airy comfort I much preferred to my Levis. The vendors would step out from behind their stalls to defend their multi-coloured pyramids of herbs, spices, fruits and vegetables. Even my barber now avoided my gaze in the mirror, and he was a Thai – a Buddhist Thai. Westerners were Westerners, whether or not their governments supported the Anglo-American coalition. I'd accepted my role of scapegoat and, in some ways, almost welcomed it.

Next morning I phoned the embassy to thank them for the dinner reception. The secretary taking my call sounded flustered. I knew better than to ask what was wrong. At the Sherlock Holmes Bar in the Gulf Hotel that night, an acquaintance told me Mme Durandard had been taken to hospital 'for her nerves'. No-one was allowed to visit, not even her husband. A few weeks later I heard she had returned to France. Alone.

My teaching stint at the kingdom's private art college finished soon afterwards, at the end of March. I was only too glad to pack my bags and escape to the relative safety of Europe now that the US and Britain had actually attacked Iraq.

On a whim, I decided to spend a week or two in Paris before heading home to Geneva-Carouge. I had friends there. And what better inspiration than the Louvre, the Centre Pompidou or simply French life with all its contradictions – the mix of piss and perfume, of catwalk chic and *clochards* in dirty alleyways, of beautiful young women and rich old men.

The Terminus Nord *brasserie* opposite the Gare du Nord is one of my all-time favourites with its stylish waiters balancing trays as easily as ballet dancers and its Art Nouveau-Art Deco interior boasting clusters and columns of lights like orbiting planets, a mosaic floor, frescos and a gleam of mirrors, framed posters, plants, mahogany, polished leather and white table-linen.

My friends and I chose *fruits de mer* for our main course. Nora and Robert have been married for ten years, but they're still so much in love they don't need to be entertained. I made conversation desultorily, savouring the crisp flesh of prawns and the ivory-smooth texture of oysters, mussels and clams while trying to eavesdrop on the couple at the table to our left. He was the size of a basketball player, late thirties, dressed in jeans and a casual checked shirt, with curly black hair, an olive complexion – and two scars that ran jaggedly across his right cheek, marring his pretty-boy features. The woman was his opposite in almost every way: a petite sleekly expensive platinum-blonde, designer-suited, well-groomed in that rich-people style which transforms even the plainest of faces into a semblance of beauty, her skin lustrous and unnaturally ageless – courtesy of Botox, no doubt. But her eyes betrayed her. It's always their eyes. She was in her mid-sixties, at least. You can't wrinkle-fill or laser away the pain of experience.

49

They had finished their main course and were sitting close together on the leather banquette, whispering. He'd put his arm around her shoulders, getting into gigolo mode. Then, quite abruptly, his voice grew louder. 'Do you love me, *Maman*?' he asked, in a tone so pleading it made me wince, and hurt – really hurt – for him. 'Please, *Maman*, tell me that you love me. *Maman*, please.' The fingers of his free hand had crept up to his scars.

The woman laughed without a crinkle around her eyes and moved out of his embrace. She slid a Dunhill from the pack on their table. 'René, *s'il te plaît!* You know I don't like to see you making a fool of yourself. Haven't I always given you money?' She snapped open a brushed silver lighter, ignoring the match he'd struck for her, and added with a careless gesture towards her monogrammed Louis Vuitton handbag, 'There's plenty more in there, don't worry.'

'But do you love me, *Maman*?' he insisted, his disfigured cheek now cupped in his hand.

'You wonder would I like you better without those cuts, maybe? Well, let me order us some dessert first.' And she waved her cigarette at a waiter hovering nearby.

I watched the son slump visibly over the menu placed in front of him.

As I strolled back to my hotel on Boulevard Magenta, having declined Nora and Robert's offer of a glass or two of Fée Verte at their place up in Montmartre, the words of the ambassador's wife insinuated themselves again, unbidden: *I don't think I've ever been moved by anything, or anyone, in my life.* The words had begun to haunt me.

What exactly had Mme Durandard meant by being 'moved'? Moved to tears, to love and affection? Moved to feeling the earth shift and whole galaxies explode? Moved to anger and disgust, to hatred even? Or moved, like René's *Maman*, to cold contempt? For a moment, I pictured the son. Instead of sitting there in slumped defeat, I imagined him straightening up and pushing away the dessert menu with sudden dignity. Imagined him calmly extracting several matches from the box, lighting them in one swift stroke and dropping them on to the pristine white table cloth in front of his mother, saying, 'Sorry, *Maman*, no Crêpe Suzette for me today,' then, just as coolly, getting up and walking out – while all hell broke loose behind him.

Smiling at the thought of it, I turned up the collar of my linen jacket. It had started to rain, a misty drizzle that in the light of the Boulevard's streetlamps shimmered satin-soft and dissolved the neon glares of shop and restaurant signs into gentle water-colours. I stared about me – and bumped into a woman who'd stopped to open her umbrella. She whirled round, staggering on high heels, her red-painted mouth ready to scream, and for one moment I thought she was the girl without a name. The girl I had sheltered in my kennel-shed almost twenty years before and who'd sneaked off afterwards without a word of thanks, leaving me alone with … with … But I didn't want to think about that. Not ever again.

By the time I'd forced the memory from my mind, the woman with the umbrella had vanished into the watercolour softness of the rain; all I could hear was the faint, wet clatter of her heels.

That night the nameless girl came back to me.

Once more I lay in the dilapidated kennel-shed above Lake Geneva, guarded by Zara the Invisible – and once more it was the eve of my thirteenth birthday.

I'd finished pretend-kissing Zara goodnight and was bur-rowing deeper into the fusty sleeping bag I'd scavenged from our cellar when I heard a loud rustle from the undergrowth to my left, where our garden merged into the Bois de Belmont. A rustle that was more than just the wind stirring the leaves or a fox after prey. Foxes don't break twigs and branches underfoot, they prowl without sound. These noises weren't made by an animal. For a moment I lay stock still, then quietly worked myself out of the sleeping bag. Curious rather than frightened, I tiptoed over to one of my spy knotholes in the wall. The noises had stopped abruptly. I caught my breath, put one eye against the hole.

The sky was overcast, but there was a purplish, floating iridescence from the full moon high above the Savoy Alps across the Lake, which muted yet illuminated everything – the rampant weeds and grass, my father's house behind the unpruned fruit trees, the other houses glistening like snails' shells in the vineyards beyond – creating a haze of unreality, of mystery and expectation. As if those veils of cloud might suddenly be pulled apart to reveal another world, another dimension, a stage set for something breathtakingly new, and terrifying.

A groan, stifled but audible. And now I see her, wearing a knee-length dress and too-bulky jacket, leaning against the apple tree ten metres away. She is holding a stick whose tip gleams like a finger bone, sharp and white. Her weapon. She is panting as if she's run a marathon. Again the groan. She's dropped the stick now and is clutching her belly.

I rush outside and through a gap in the fence. The girl's mouth opens in a silent scream. I reach her just as she falls down in a faint. I kneel beside her. That's when the moon comes out. Fifteen at most, with a straggle of dark hair. Her face, hands and bare legs look as cold and pale as marble. The hem of her dress is muddy and wet, probably from the wayward stream that slinks through the wood.

Another groan and her eyes flick open. 'No!' she shouts. Then again, 'No! No!'

I have to clap a hand over her mouth or she'll wake everyone – my father, my grandmother, the neighbours.

She claws at me.

'Hey,' I say, shaking my head to make her stop, 'I'm just a kid. I'm called Maurice and this is our garden.' I smile to reassure her, but she only starts panting more rapidly, as if getting ready to grab her stick and take off.

Then she says, 'Can I … stay here awhile?'

Inside the shed, she began whimpering and screaming and

thrashing about. I gave her an old cushion to bite on for the pain.

I never thought there could be so much blood, so much smelly, gooey stuff inside a girl like her, so young. The baby was the size of a very small loaf of bread and seemed to slither out all by itself. It never moved, never made a sound, and despite the cloud shadows, I could see its unblinking eyes staring and staring until I covered the poor thing with a rag.

'Boy or girl?' Her voice was high. 'No, don't tell me, Maurice. I didn't want it, anyway!'

When she finally dozed off, exhausted, I kept murmuring to her, kept inhaling her body odours, her sweat and blood and worse, kept listening to her breathing, kept holding her arm as it twitched in her sleep and, for a dare, kept licking the tears off her cheeks.

I woke at dawn, and she was gone. No goodbye. No nothing.

I buried the tiny body (a boy's) and the afterbirth under a copper beech in the middle of the wood, having dug down deep into the loose earth so the predators wouldn't find them. The sun was rising, its rays slanting through the trees, bringing them alive in translucent shades of green that quivered into substance as the light flowed and played and mingled with birdsong. The sun was rising, and I was thirteen years old.

The nightmare memory had made me cry as usual, hot spurts of tears that scalded my cheeks and left sore, red streaks. How I wished now I had accepted my friends' offer of some Fée Verte the previous evening – at least then I could have blamed the absinthe for blindsiding me.

I threw open the hotel window, grateful for once to be assaulted by traffic fumes and the bright glare and noise of an early Paris morning. Only April, and getting hot already. I leant my elbows on the windowsill, squinted down through the tracery of leaves into the boulevard. A young boy with a baguette under one arm was chasing after a nimble white dog that had mastered the art of running and cocking a leg simultaneously. A window cleaner emptied his bucket into the gutter. A couple of old women stood talking with their noses nearly touching. I remained at the window for a long time.

And yet it was thanks to the nameless girl that I became what I am now: an artist, a sculptor. I started with earth and mud, inspired by the bare-handed digging I'd done in the woods. But the resulting figures, crude and gnome-like, disintegrated almost as soon as they were finished, crumbling back into the ground – dust to dust, ashes to ashes. They were superseded by semi-permanent charcoal drawings, scrawls really, on the shed walls and, when I ran out of space, on the floorboards. After that I began to experiment with crayons, watercolours, glow-in-the-dark paints, acrylics, oils – whatever my pocket money could buy at Jallut's or Krieg's, my favourite fine art shops in Lausanne. The shed was my first atelier-cum-gallery, its surfaces a palimpsest of ghostly renderings of the girl and the gory stillbirth, and of my own absent mother. Painting was a compulsion, a kind of exorcism. I used a lot of visceral reds; I'd read somewhere that the human kidney filters the equivalent of a whole bathtub's worth of blood a day.

Before I left for the Ecole Supérieure des Beaux-Arts in Geneva, where I later taught sculpture, I overpainted everything in the shed with creosote. Last time I visited my father, the shed was still standing, preserved in its decrepitude like an old drunk with his insides pickled by alcohol.

Having a shave in the hotel's stuffy shower room, I switched on the TV to snap out of the past and caught the tail-end of a breaking news item about Iraq – the toppling of the massive statue of Saddam Hussein in central Baghdad. I laid down my razor on the writing desk. Then, half my face still covered in lather, I watched mesmerised as the colossus of stone was attached to a metal rope by US soldiers and pulled down flat on its back while a crowd of Iraqi men went wild, jeering and chanting, dancing on the effigy's head, the uniformed chest and loins, hitting it with their shoes, screaming at it, kicking it, hacking it to pieces and, joined now by women and children, hauling the severed head in chains through the streets of the city. I sat down heavily on the bed.

The following year I spent almost entirely in my atelier in Carouge, the Greenwich Village of Geneva. No more teaching for me. The money I'd earned in the Middle East had been tax-free and I'd saved most of it. This was my chance.

Out of all the possible materials I might have chosen – plaster of Paris, clay, wood, papier-mâché, wax, wool, leather, fabrics, plastics, polystyrene, resins, glass, fibreglass, metals – I went for wood and animal hides, the latter's pungency biting right through my life, back to my childhood.

I hardly ate. Worked late into the night, my nose, mouth and eyes clogging up with sawdust as I fanatically, furiously, chopped, chiselled, sanded and hammered away at a number of large birch logs I'd had delivered by tractor. Every so often the words of the ambassador's wife would go through my head – *I don't think I've ever been moved by anything, or anyone, in my life* – and I'd drive myself all the harder.

I never even allowed my best friend and fellow sculptor Jean-Luc into my atelier. Nor my recent girlfriend Gina, a sociology student and self-proclaimed 'post-neo-feminist'. We'd met at Bains des Pâquis, one of Geneva's lakeside swimming pools, on a summer day too hot for work. I'd been lying on the beach gazing over at the *jet d'eau* and its rainbow refractions when she ran out of the water and, laughing, shook herself all over me.

By December I had a total of sixteen free-standing frame-figures, ranging in height from one and a half to over three metres. 'Salome' was the tallest, and my *pièce de résistance*.

Just before Valentine's Day I finished the wet-formation of the leather, having stretched the slippery skins so tightly across the wooden frames they resembled creatures exhumed from Irish peat bogs. By mid-April the sculptures were dried out, partly varnished but still vulnerable enough for my purposes, and presenting themselves in various stages of *déshabillé*. The real secret, of course, lay sealed inside them.

A week or so after I'd added the finishing touches, a nipple ring here, a lacy ruffle or an ankle chain there, I invited Gina and Jean-Luc round for a trial run in my secluded atelier garden. I sacrificed one of the less accomplished male figures. The effects were quite stunning, made even more so by Gina's shocked tears and Jean-Luc's open envy. If the very act of destruction could create art, then hatred might be resurrected as love, and mere motion turn into emotion.

By the end of the next month the invitations for the *vernissage* of 'I Call Her Salome' had been sent out and the publicity was in full swing, with notices in newspapers and art shop windows, website postings and a blitz of email alerts. Wishing in vain I could contact René's *Maman*, the nameless girl or my mother (if indeed she was still alive), I made do with Mme Durandard, whose address in a wealthy suburb of Paris I'd tracked down with the help of my friends in Montmartre. I wanted to meet her one more time. Wanted to continue our conversation, pre-wineglass, as it were. Wanted to ask her what her life felt like now, whether she had finally ascended into the exalted ranks of those who have learnt to be 'moved'.

There were more than a hundred guests present that night, drinking champagne under the chestnut trees in the cobbled yard behind Galerie Sauvage, not far from my atelier. It was the beginning of June and a sultry evening darkened by purple-black thunderclouds pushing down over Mont Salève. The sculptures to be 're-created' had been placed on plastic sheeting at strategic points around the yard.

When I produced the pistol (for which I'd got a special permit from the police, just in case), people gasped and instinctively pressed closer together, breaking away from me like a herd of frightened cattle. I brandished the gun in the air with a laugh. '*Courage, mes amis!*'

The first sculpture was a bony old man with a small, shrivelled penis and blind-looking eyes. But I felt no release. Not when I pulled the trigger. Not when the shot rang out. Not when the bags of red paint burst, spraying the tattered leather torso with spectacular blood patterns as it slowly keeled over. My guests clapped themselves into a frenzy, shouting for more. More shots, more blood, more destruction. Then came the figure of a girl with a bloated belly and pierced nipples. Her body didn't quite explode, just split gracefully open from stomach to heart, dripping red. The applause died down to a ripple. A few women began to walk away, glancing back at me over their shoulders and muttering abuse. Most people stood motionless, their eyes transfixed by the torn belly and blood-coloured splashes. Suddenly I heard Gina yell, 'Fuck you, Maurice!'

That's when I shot 'Salome' – half man-eating praying mantis, half Helen of Troy – shot her three times, once in the head, once in the heart, once in the abdomen, shot her at such close range I ended up splattered with paint myself. Towering above me, shredded to bits, 'Salome' tilted ever so slightly to one side.

I looked for Mme Durandard, looked and looked. But I couldn't see her. I was sure she was there. She had to be. If not in the flesh, then in spirit. This was my moment of triumph and I needed to share it with her. Not that she would be clapping, of course. She wouldn't be the kind of woman to give praise easily. Instead she would slowly turn towards me, lay her long, cool white fingers on my chest, over my heart, and gently move them up and down and across the way, smearing the blood-red paint all over me and herself, her face as grave and serene as a child's.

The angry furore and the controversy over my 'misogynist, psychopath *vernissage*' soon spread and there were articles in all the major newspapers, reports on the radio and on TV, blogs and chat-room discussions on the internet. The picture of 'Salome' and me acquired iconic status. Most arts correspondents interpreted my 'show' as a legitimate, truly artistic outcry against the ravages of armed conflict perpetrated against the innocent.

Ever since, I have been inundated with commissions. People like playing at war in their own backyards, it seems, and are prepared to pay good money for it. I have exhibited in London, New York and Amsterdam. The Centre Pompidou is next. I have hangers-on now, and groupies. I receive fan mail, hate mail, begging letters. Sometimes I kiss my hands, finger by finger, starting with the pearl-pink crescent moon of each nail, to thank them for existing, and for giving me an existence.

I still haven't heard from Mme Durandard, but I live in hope. After all, the heart beats a hundred thousand times a day.

Invisible Partners

Towards dusk I often go and sit in the church. A walk along windswept pavements with slabs so uneven I have to lift my feet up high. Like wading on solid ground. Once I fell and hurt my knee and now whenever I try to hurry, the pain is like a brake pad cutting through my joint.

I am fond of this church. Its simplicity is so different from the baroque excesses I was used to as a child, decades ago, in my own country. There are no knick-knacks here, just glass and stone and wood. A heraldic ceiling and pews of pitch pine, stone pillars without carvings, a stone arch with three stained-glass windows and, to the left, several dark shadows like sweat marks in the shape of something. People say it's a ghost. Sometimes, they say, you can see its heart beating; then the wall begins to vibrate and there are flickers of light and harsh scraping noises like the grinding of millstones.

How I have prayed to catch a glimpse of that ghost! Just for the sake of action, and a flare of life beyond the grave. Not that I'm particularly religious. Our wedding ceremony over, Jim didn't leave me much leisure to commune with God – or with myself, for that matter – between getting me pregnant and installing me behind the counter of his grocer's shop.

Now, of course, they're all long gone: the children, Jim, the generations of mice in the storeroom and the cats that chased them.

Late last night the phone rang, the first time since my birthday at the weekend. Static, screeches and howls greeted me and I knew at once it was Michael, intrepid wanderer, photojournalist and heartbreaker.

'Sorry about the racket, Mum,' he cried. 'I'm in the middle of the Amazon rainforest. How are you?'

'Son, good to hear from you. I thought you'd forgotten me.' A half-laugh. Truth was, he had forgotten my birthday. (Unlike his younger twin sisters, with their dutiful calls from Zurich and Geneva, their flowers, chocolates and family snaps.) 'Trust me, Michael,' I added, my laughter a little more grating now, 'I'm as fine as I shall ev–'

Another screech, sounding much closer.

'Wow, that was a blue and yellow macaw! Beautiful birds, Mum, you'd love them!'

Michael's enthusiasm was genuine – genuinely juvenile in a man of forty-six.

I told him I'd seen a macaw before. At the zoo. Much safer for everyone concerned, wouldn't he say?

I'd not changed one bit, he exclaimed. 'Still your pugnacious old self!'

Against a background of ear-piercing shrieks, I asked when he'd be back in Scotland.

'Next summer, probably. Got some unfinished business.'

No need to inquire any further. Wherever he went, Michael's path was littered with broken hearts. Not for the first time I found myself wondering whether, in addition to my five carefully accounted-for Swiss grandchildren, there were others scattered across the globe, nameless and of all colours, ages and religions, with my son's grey eyes. That's when the static on the line grew suddenly unbearable.

The leaves in the churchyard scrunch under my feet and I imagine the dead whispering among themselves as they feel me passing above.

Seventy-one, seventy-one, seventy-one, they're saying, *quite a few years yet until she joins us.*

I thrust my head out and push into the breeze with deliberate exaggeration, letting my coat-tails flap wildly as I show off my new navy blue shoes with the Velcro fasteners (my own birthday treat to myself). Halfway to the church porch I have to stop for a moment to regain my breath, one hand on a gravestone for support. After all, I don't intend to arrive within those spectral walls puffing like an ancient locomotive. The walk has tired me rather more than usual; my back is aching and my knee about to seize up.

'Regular exercise won't do you any harm, Rosa, provided you take it easy,' my GP said only last week, writing out the new prescription for my painkillers.

'You know I'm a tough old bird, Doctor,' I replied with a resonant laugh – though perhaps it was merely a loud cackle, the cackle of a silly old bird.

Now, leaning harder on the gravestone, I repeat, 'Silly old bird, silly old bird.'

Around me the afternoon is all blue and tarnished gold, and I ignore the drunken shouts from a nearby pub.

I've always been a bit of a talker, to be honest. At the shop this was an asset; most of the customers liked a few minutes' chit-chat or gossip, especially if it came in a lilting foreign accent. At home Jim used to complain, saying I was worse than the radio – no off-button. After his death I carried on talking, in a mish-mash of Swiss German and English, to all the empty rooms in the flat, sometimes even to the woman in the mirror, watching the lines in her face deepen and her hair turn silver. It gives me a thrill to feel my lips and tongue moving, slowly or rapidly, depending on my mood, and the bursts of air from my mouth prove I'm still alive.

My fingers have begun to trace the badly eroded surface of the gravestone, along the crumbling grooves of some letters. 'RIP,' I hear myself murmur. 'Whoever you are.'

There's a sharp rustle to my right and the black and white flash of a single magpie as it flies up into one of the sycamores. Chattering angrily, it starts crashing about the foliage.

'Rosie! No! Don't!' A woman's voice.

I jerk round. Not many people call me Rosie here, only a few friends from the Swiss Club and Gary and Stephen, my neighbours.

At first I can't see anyone. Then I notice a bow-legged bull terrier doing its business next to a marble gravestone. Slowly it angles its head to stare over at me from small pig eyes. The metal spikes on its collar glint in the low slanting rays of the sun. Taking my chance, I sidle off, with vague, pacifying gestures, towards the safety of the church.

Leaves, broken twigs and feathers drift down from the sycamore, chased by shrill bird cries.

'Sorry!' A young woman has appeared at my elbow. She is as pale as death and there are two silver rings in her nostrils. 'I didn't mean to disturb you. Rosie can be such a naughty wee thing.' She smiles indulgently, then bends to pat the dog that has ambled up to her, its fat pink tongue lolling like a bacon rasher.

For a moment I am reminded of myself, years ago, holding little Michael's hand and popping a peppermint cream into his mouth as I apologise yet again for one of his pranks. When the girl straightens up, my hand is curled around empty air.

'That's okay,' I say. 'I thought you meant me, you see.'

'Pardon?' The girl's lips are painted an odd shade of purplish black and her short-cropped hair has the look of wet tar. She isn't naturally pale, I realise now and quickly glance away, mumbling, 'Well, I'm also…'

But she is already walking off. 'I'd better pick that up,' she calls over her shoulder.

The bull terrier sniffs my new shoes, from toes to heels and back again, before nosing along the tails of my raincoat.

I stand rigid, try counting to ten. Four, five, six –

The bald, pink snout nudges my left shin.

I smile down at it uneasily. A nasty-looking animal. 'Good dog,' I quaver, avoiding the pig eyes.

The snout inspects my other shin, releasing hot, meaty exhalations up the inside of my leg.

'Shoo now, shoo,' I mutter and set off casually, pretending to stroll rather than run-and-stall towards the church porch; the bull terrier trots by my side, panting.

'Rosie?'

The dog stops at once and so do I, quite instinctively.

'Rosie! Here!' The girl has vanished among the gravestones and briars.

Swivelling its head in my direction every few steps, the dog finally slinks off and I sigh with relief, then continue my way up onto the porch.

As I reach for the brass door handle into my sanctuary, I become aware again of the drunken shouts from before. They sound louder now, nearer – and that's when I catch sight of a group of young people gathered at the bottom of the churchyard in the late afternoon sun. Dressed in black like mourners, with mops of green, orange and blue hair, they're lounging on the tombs, smoking and gulping from big plastic cider bottles. Three girls have started a chant-and-dance around a Celtic cross. Like straggly crows they flap their arms, skip, lurch and strut. Now some of the men give chase while the others cheer them on with yells and wolf-whistles and the bull terrier barks excitedly. One girl ends up getting brandished about in the air, pummelling her assailant's black leather jacket, kicking and squealing. The rest of them shriek and howl. Friends indeed!

I brace myself, ready to make a limping rush towards the girl with the words, I'll help you if no-one else will! – when I see her being laid down on a tomb behind some bushes and, perfectly quiet and docile now, pulling up her T-shirt to let Leather Jacket fondle her breasts.

Suddenly, the shouts and screams and giggles are more than I can take. Much more. Worse than the din of Michael's rainforest.

There's no-one else in the church. Only me, the wooden pews, the stained glass with its fading images of the Crucifixion on the stone floor – and the marks on the wall. I sit down in the front row and try to concentrate on them. But it's hard to shut out the noise from the churchyard. I want to see the ghost. I must see it. Now.

'NOW! NOW! NOW!'

The loud viciousness of my voice makes me jump. I clap

a hand to my mouth and slip the scarf over my ears. Flitting shadows have begun to weave across the windows outside; more magpies, no doubt. Dizzy, I gaze up at the heraldic ceiling. Straight above me is a perfectly carved red heart. I am a sane person, I tell myself, I don't need ghosts.

Just then there's a gust of wind that tugs my scarf loose. The heavy door falls into the lock with a bump. Footsteps and low murmurings. I ignore them. Real worshippers, probably, praying in muted tones.

All at once, hysterical laughter fills the nave. 'See the ghost? It's bloody moving!'

'Hey, pipe down.'

'No shit, Geoff, it *is* moving! Look!'

'Forget about it, okay.' A pause, followed by a creak. 'There now. That's better, isn't it?'

But *I* still can't see anything. No vibrations. No flickers of light. Nothing. NOTHING. The same old marks cover the same old patches of wall. And the scraping noises, clearly those of wood on stone, come from the back of the church.

I get to my feet abruptly and stumble towards the door.

Their black-clad bodies are almost indistinguishable from the pew on which they're lying. Their faces are turned towards me, chalky blurs in the twilight except for the silver gleams of the girl's nose-rings. A growl sounds from underneath them as the bull terrier shifts its bulk.

'Stay, Rosie!' the girl hisses, and stupidly I stop. Stand quite still. Until I feel their eyes on me, glaring, so I make a show of rearranging my scarf and buttoning the coat up to my chin before braving the world outside. I have my birthday shoes – they'll carry me home safely enough.

Next morning I get up late. Dark rain runs like spittle down the windows; the trees whine in the wind. I know I'll have to trudge round to the deli again for one of their sugar-glazed *pains aux raisins*. When I was pregnant with Michael, I developed a lifelong craving for raisins, which always grows worse during weather like this.

The shop assistant smiles on seeing me enter with my big, black, man's umbrella. 'The usual, is it, Mrs Harrower?' she asks. 'Something sweet for a dreich day?'

'Oh yes, please.' I smile back, then watch her pick out the largest of the pastries. 'At the rate I eat them, you'd think life was all dreichness...' I finish with a little shrug and the assistant gives the required chuckle as she rings up the till.

The *Herald & Post* is waiting on the doormat, faintly damp. I place it on the kitchen radiator while I grind some luxury-roast coffee beans from Brazil (bought yesterday after my phone call with Michael, on the spur of a sentimental moment). By the time the cafetière is ready, the newspaper has crisped up again and I carry everything through to the living room, where I settle in my favourite armchair.

Then I open the paper, saving the personal ads for last, as a treat. I can spend hours guessing at the real people behind the words, imagining how the 'romantic, fun-and-nature-loving academic in his prime' who wishes to meet 'slim, intelligent blonde between 30 and 35' might actually be a divorced teacher of retirement age with a penchant for hiking and watching sunsets among clouds of midges. I grin to myself, savouring the bitterness of the coffee on my tongue. As I glance through the pages, I uncoil my *pain aux raisins* and tear off bite-sized chunks. The raisins have a slightly burnt taste today, as if the baker had forgotten his pastries in the oven and only just managed to rescue them.

And all of a sudden I hear myself say, 'Enough simply isn't enough, Rosie – it's too little. Too little bustle, too little company, too little sunshine. Not much of a life.'

I'm still swallowing the soft snake-belly centre of the pastry when I find myself standing by the phone, clutching a page of the newspaper. My index finger has started to tap out a number and I can't seem to make it stop: I am ringing a removal firm.

A removal firm?

The advertisement must have caught my attention unawares – or 'subconsciously', as Michael would have said. It's so big, a third of a page nearly, and has two happily grinning stickmen balancing whole tables and beds on the palms of their hands. One's even got a birdcage on his head. Silly old bird, silly old bird, an inner voice cautions me. But with a chortling sense of release I realise that, yes, that's what I want. I want to go off. Want to go away.

'Caledonian Removals, Moira speaking. What's the name and address, please?'

I give her the details: the size of the flat, number of bedrooms, types of furniture, special items like pictures and plants and the dusty old spinning wheel I inherited from my mother, valuables, breakables, the lot. I'm beginning to enjoy myself. I'm going to go off. I'm going to go away. Michael will be amazed.

But then the woman inquires about my new address and her question brings me down to earth with a vengeance. I have to go *somewhere*. Going in itself isn't enough. I need a destination. An aim. Always this word. It drove me away from home when I was only eighteen. Drove me all over Switzerland, via France to England and finally to Scotland – and into Jim's eager, grabbing arms. Drove me to become who I am. *Aim. Aim. Aim.*

'Aim high, Rosie. Don't lower your sights unless you have to. Remember that,' my father's teacherly voice used to exhort me. A stern man, despite the sweet smell of his pipe. Leaning forward in his padded leather chair until I'd nod.

So now, on an impulse, I reply with girlish airiness, 'Oh, didn't I mention it? I'm going abroad.'

Instead of asking, 'Where abroad?' which I expect and dread for I really have no idea, the woman says briskly, 'Sorry, we don't do abroad. You'd better try elsewhere. Continental –'

She has started to sound impatient, and I don't blame her. Though perhaps she is merely jealous of me. Perhaps she has children who still need their mother. Still need fed and clothed and sheltered. Need their beds. Their little chests of drawers and trunks spilling toys all over the floor. Their Play Stations, their iPods, their clutter.

After hanging up, I slowly move into the centre of the room and lift my arms for an invisible partner to hold me. I shuffle my feet to the melody of an old-fashioned waltz. I can hear it quite clearly in my head.

'Because You Foreign'

She watched them make their entrance wreathed in smoke, devils reeking of sulphur and sin. The first was black and sang falsetto. He was sporting a chiffon robe, enormous breasts and a pouch that barely concealed his crotch.

Maggie turned away. She shouldn't have come here. Shouldn't have given in to George yet again. She could see him grinning towards the stage, one elbow propped on the cocktail table between them, shoulders swaying lazily to the beat. Sparks flew from the tip of his cigarette, which flared like a fiery eye.

She shouldn't have followed him to Tenerife at all. But after two months of being alone in cold, rain-sodden Scotland while he toured the Canaries for his new Guidebook, she'd been ripe for persuasion. Had even agreed to stay in his mangy old army tent, 'his home from home', to experience the wilderness he was always raving about. And now she'd tagged along like a damn puppy so he could 'research' the island's club scene… At least they would be staying at a hotel tonight; the hordes of lizards, spiders and cockroaches scuttling around the coastal hills were welcome to the tent.

Staring at the vomit-yellow banana liqueur George had ordered for her, Maggie was reminded again of this morning. They'd been woken by the dawn chorus, and George had unzipped the warm cocoon of her sleeping bag…

A Madonna lookalike was strutting across the stage on three-inch heels, fondling his microphone like a karaoke singer during the rutting season. Maggie winced.

Crawling in beside her, George had called her his 'sweet little baby girl' – as if their row last night had never happened, as if he'd never accused her of being a 'pathetic toddler with no initiative'. Well, the 'sweet little baby girl' hadn't forgotten, and had felt her stomach heave. She'd only just managed to fumble open the tent flap and rush outside. A spurt of bile had hit the saddle of George's mountain bike tethered to a fig tree. She'd wiped it clean with the hem of her T-shirt, but he'd sworn at her. Shouted she was undermining him, then pedalled off down the track in a cloud of dust, blasting past almond trees and prickly pears studded with angry red fruit.

Hours later he had returned, hot, sweaty and triumphant. 'I've killed two birds with one stone,' he announced. 'For the next few days we'll combine work' – he indicated himself – 'and holidays' – he nodded at her. 'We'll be staying at the Palmera. What do you think?'

She had accepted, too lost and lonely not to.

Maggie forced down a sip of the banana liqueur. It was luke-warm, but surprisingly unsyrupy, and she had some more. When a waiter passed with a bowl of ice cubes, she motioned to him, tossing her blonde curls. He stopped at once. Smiled down into her cleavage – she'd chosen to wear the tight, low-cut number as a concession to George (or was it perhaps another sign of admitting defeat?). For a moment, as the waiter bent over her, she could feel his breath in her hair. Glancing up, she saw his lips part and the tip of his tongue flick briefly against the white of his teeth.

It would be so easy, she told herself, so easy just to up and go. Her whole life she'd wavered. And waited. Waited for the surge of courage that surely must come at some point, like a hidden switch being flipped inside, to do her own thing and not let herself be beholden to anyone any more.

George was blowing smoke rings. He seemed absorbed in the action on stage, where yet another performer, this one in a pink lamé dress slit to the hips, kept shaking his smoothly shaved arms to flaunt a set of golden wings.

Maggie got to her feet so violently she banged into the table. George half-turned in his seat. 'Some show this, isn't it, baby?' he said and winked at her, squashing out his cigarette. As if for the first time she noticed how red and fleshy his lips were, how lime-green his eyes. Then he caught her by the wrist and tugged her towards him until his head was rubbing up against her breasts.

Maggie stiffened. She hated him doing this, especially in public, and she knew he knew – she'd told him often enough. When his hand gripped her buttocks, she wrenched herself free.

'Sorry, George, I need to go to the loo.' She faked a smile and scooped up her small rucksack. 'Back shortly.' She could tell he was annoyed. But so was she. And she'd no idea what she was going to do next.

Seconds later she got entangled in a boisterous group of Spanish girls on their way to the door, each with a bulging plastic bag. Giggling drunkenly, their faces shiny with melting make-up, they simply pulled her along, out into the night.

'Hey!' Maggie protested. 'Let go of me.'

'No worry! No worry!' they said with dark, long 'o's and rolling 'r's and patted her on the back.

For an instant she resisted. But the soft, indigo air felt soothing, thick as it was with the sweet-and-sour smells from a nearby Chinese restaurant and the drifting scent of oleander blossoms. She could hear George's voice: *Pathetic toddler.* What if the girls were robbers, their bags full of loot? Or kidnappers in disguise? From across the street, beyond the elephant-skin palm trees, came the sounds of the Atlantic lashing the rocks – a relentless pounding that seemed to her the only thing she could trust.

They halted under a streetlamp and the girls crowded round. One of them, tall, gaunt, with large, liquid eyes, said in heavily accented English, 'Party for women, before marry.' She paused, gestured towards a plump girl in an off-the-shoulder silver ruffle dress and silver sandals: 'Consuela, the bride.'

Maggie smiled uncertainly. Perhaps she should just congratulate Consuela, then make her excuses. She didn't belong. And she didn't want to. Didn't. Didn't. Didn't. She wasn't a toddler, goddammit, or a puppy. She put out a hand to push through. And suddenly they were all introducing themselves, the Carmens, Martas, Teresas, Esmeraldas, Lolas and Marías. Their dusky, exuberant voices left her quite giddy. Here were complete strangers, more than a dozen of them, who wanted her to be with them, wanted her to share their fun.

As they strolled along under the shadows of palm and rubber trees, past open-air restaurants, thudding neon-lit bars, the termite structures of hotels and apartment blocks, the girls asked where she was from, was she on holidays, and what about a boy-friend? She did her best to answer them truthfully, more or less.

They had just crossed the avenue towards some steps that seemed to follow the shoreline to the next resort when Maggie's curiosity finally got the better of her and, indicating the plastic bags, she said: 'Your swimming costumes?'

The girls' laughter silenced the cicadas. 'For picnic,' they replied. 'You like eat?' Maggie nodded, feeling relieved. And vaguely disappointed. Why had they dragged her along? But then again, why not? As if to reassure her, the cicadas resumed their shrilling.

'Vamonos!' the gaunt girl with the large eyes called out and they started to climb the steeply rising steps in single file. Cast-iron lampposts glowed at intervals. The air was a loose piece of silk brushing against Maggie's bare legs and arms. A wild cat screamed from the scrub, a thin, unearthly wail that stopped almost as suddenly as it had begun. Below them the Atlantic kept thundering against the cavernous volcanic rocks, but now the never-endingness of the onslaught made Maggie shiver. The steps snaked round a corner, dipped sharply and levelled out.

One of the two Esmeraldas, with hair longer than her mini-skirt, waved a cigarette at the black shapes rearing up in the distance. 'Please to meet Los Gigantes,' she said and chuckled throatily.

The cliffs really did resemble giants. Maggie could just about distinguish the mass of white horses at their base and, to the west, the thin seam where the star-littered sky joined the ocean.

Someone touched her hand. 'You come. No shoes.' Consuela's teeth shone in the dark. The silver sandals dangled from her fingers. Maggie's instinct told her to run. Run away from these bossy strangers, away from the stony aloofness of the giants.

Instead she found herself bending meekly to undo her ankle straps. The other girls had disappeared one by one down the side of the path.

There were more steps here, cut into the near-sheer rock face and descending to what looked like a breakwater, a sheltered pool walled off from the sea in a perfect semicircle. Spindrift glistened whenever a bigger wave – every seventh, wasn't it? – crashed over and roiled the surface. Maggie moved carefully, probing the ground toes first, down towards the moonlight reflected in the water.

The moment they reached the bottom, several torches burst into flame, illuminating a black rockscape of frozen lava, no sand. Here and there bath towels were spread over the boulders. An acrid smell of burning hung in the air from the fire that was being coaxed alight further along. Every girl seemed to have her appointed task. Everyone except her and Consuela, who was standing quite still now, staring out at the white-crested waves beyond the breakwater, a fluorescent silver figure in a charred landscape.

Bottles began to pop. One, two, three… Maggie lost count. Then she was given a paper cup filled to the brim with Cava.

'*Salud!*' The girls converged on the bride. '*Salud*, Consuela!'

Maggie was about to have a sip when she heard a shout and saw the gaunt girl tilt a bottle of Cava right over Consuela's head. Consuela shrieked, ducked. Too late. The contents of the bottle streamed down her face like tears, fizzed along her bare shoulders, soaked into the ruffle dress. Someone had grabbed hold of her now and the Carmens, Martas, Teresas, Esmeraldas, Lolas and Marías gave cat whistles as another bottle was upended. And another. Shriek by shriek, Consuela wriggled her generous body a little less until, half-laughing, she yielded and opened her mouth obligingly to catch a gulp. The fabric of the dress clung to her in a wet embrace.

All at once, Esmeralda of the Miniskirt beckoned to Maggie and, handing her two flaring torches, directed her to a rock shaped like a throne by the side of the pool.

'What's going on?'

'No worry. Sit here,' Esmeralda said in her guttural drawl.

The girls had started to throw their paper cups at Consuela: 'Salud! Salud! Salud!' Some of them now pounced on her, pulled and pushed her into the sea. Dunked her. When Consuela came up for air, coughing and snorting, they cheered.

'Imbéciles!' Consuela spluttered, shoving armfuls of water at them. The girls cheered, shouted things Maggie didn't understand. Anger was boiling up inside her. She'd had it with being told what to do and tagging along, a witness to other people's fun. And she wasn't a goddamn candlestick!

She'd show them.

She raised the torches, ready to toss them into the water, anticipating their wild-cat hiss – when, at that very moment, she glimpsed a sleek grey shadow leap across the moon-spangled waves, far out at sea. Then leap again. And again. Pirouetting with effortless grace. And suddenly it felt like she herself was leaping with it – leaping and whipping up spray as she joined in its solitary dance. Together the two of them arced through the soft night air, together they dived into the cool of the ocean, they arced and dived, arced and dived as one. After their highest, most spectacular leap, Maggie closed her eyes as though letting herself sink into the pulsating waters, deeper and deeper. And even when she sensed that the last ray of moonlight would have long since broken like a too-taut string of pearls, leaving behind only darkness, she wasn't afraid.

Her eyes flew open as something burnt her thighs; she was holding the torches dangerously tilted and the hot wax had dripped a foreign script all over her throne of rock.

There were yells and screams and splashes. The girls were all in the pool now, dressed only in their underwear. They'd caught Consuela and, undeterred by her flailings and thrashings, were peeling off the silver ruffle dress like an old skin. Then they struck up a marching tune and carried her ashore.

Later, seated on the rocks around the fire, the girls tried to explain to Maggie why they had brought her with them. A good-luck charm, they appeared to be saying as they chewed, smoked and swung their legs in time to a CD.

'Because you foreign.' Nibbling a piece of freshly grilled goat's cheese. Biting into a wrinkly, salt-encrusted potato. Licking some *mojo* off thumb and forefinger.

'Because you blonde.' Inhaling deeply, exhaling with a sigh.

'And you very pretty.' Heels bashing the boulders to keep up with 'Me and Bobby McGee'.

Maggie just smiled and shook her head, then had a big, heart-stopping gulp of sangria.

She arrived at the Palmera long after midnight and nearly stumbled into the purple-flowering oleander by the entrance. The key was still on its hook in Reception. George was no doubt amusing himself without her – the way he'd done before she flew in three days ago and the way he'd do once she'd left again, a week from now. Maggie grimaced as she unlocked the door. The room felt stifling hot and she opened both windows, lingering briefly. From the restaurant downstairs came flamenco rhythms pierced by laughter. On the balcony below, a couple lay groping and groaning.

George's *knock-knock-knock* jerked her awake.

'Where have you been?' he exclaimed when she opened the door. 'I've been looking all over for you – in restaurants, bars, discos.'

His feet slapped across the tiles to the bathroom and she followed him, glancing at his eyes in the mirror. They were bloodshot, with a wary, irritated glitter.

'I felt so tired suddenly. Couldn't bear another minute in that club ...' Her voice trailed off into a yawn. For an instant she imagined herself back with the dolphin again. Leaping over the seventh wave, so much fiercer, deadlier and more beautiful than the other six.

'What are you smiling at?' she heard George say. He had finished washing and was standing there stark naked, watching her with suspicion.

'Nothing,' she replied.

Up here on the slopes of the volcano, life receded. Maggie breathed in the air, which was pure and rarefied, sharply cold in her lungs. An icy wind chiselled indiscriminately at the exposed flesh of tourists, lava boulders, chunks of snow, the stained concrete shell of the cable-car station. She was grateful for her fleece, sweater and jeans, though they'd been a damn nuisance down below, in that sun-baked wasteland where, George said, *Star Wars* had been filmed and which he had insisted on trekking through, to give her a 'flavour of the desert'. Four and a half hours of stony ochres, reds, mauves, bluish-greens and greys, of endless pumice pellets, disfigured volcanic rocks and scrawny shrubs had certainly achieved that.

Because George suffered from asthma, he'd decided against riding up in the cable car and instead pressed his Nikon on her, saying he needed pictures for the Guide: 'The volcano, the lava, the smoke holes, the view – from every angle. It's important, Maggie. Don't mess up, okay?' His red lips had smiled at her, his lime-green eyes hidden behind sunglasses.

Now that she was here, after queuing for over an hour, she felt cheated. She'd expected more than this jumble of dirty-brown clods that masqueraded as earth yet were rock-hard, more than these patches of pristine snow and ice. Much more. She'd been hoping for deepest devil blackness. Like the hellish charredness of the beach last night. The least she could do was climb to the summit – surely there'd be signs of heat and fire up there?

Crossing the viewing terrace, she approached the roped-off path and was about to jump over when a guard with mirrored sunglasses strode up and waved his arms at her.

'*No pasar,*' he growled.

Maggie pulled a face and turned away. Then, abruptly, she

spun round, camera at the ready. *Click*. Catching him with his mouth open.

In the hazy distance, beyond the crater rim of what must have once been a volcano of colossal proportions, she could make out the sea and, on the horizon, the faint blue outline of Gran Canaria.

With the summit off-limits, she followed the short trail around the mountain flank. Just as she was passing a family, a terrible stench hit her. The children were laughing and holding their noses.

'That's the sulphur,' their father told them.

Maggie noticed a plume of vapour escaping from a nearby cleft and slowed down, raised the camera, waited. *Click*. A clandestine close-up of the family as they scrambled over the rocks to investigate. She walked on.

Fake and desolation, she kept thinking, everything on this island was either one or the other. The moonscapes of dead, burnt-out matter. The volcano puffing smoke, yet apparently harmless enough for cable cars to hoist tourists up and down its side all day long. The south coast, shrouded in mist, with its beaches of golden sand shipped from the Sahara.

Having reached the end of the trail, she could distinguish the soft double hump of La Palma in the pale blue wash of the Atlantic and, to the left, far beyond the craggy mouth of another peak, the rounded back of La Gomera. The two islands looked like living creatures of the sea. But that, too, was an illusion.

She was putting away the camera when someone asked: 'How about a photo?'

'What?' Maggie glanced up.

A group of pierced and painted teenagers had stopped beside her and one of them, a girl with flame-coloured hair and rings through her eyebrows, now repeated, 'A photo, of you.'

For a moment Maggie stared, then she smiled. 'Why not,' she said. 'Yeah, thanks, that's a great idea.' Growing enthusiastic, she added with a laugh, 'But first I'll take some of you.'

Twice already George had gone to the small shop for the volcano pictures, and twice the owner had shaken his head: '*Lo siento, señor.* Next day.' Hand on heart.

'Okay, *mañana.*' He'd given a sharp nod to express his displeasure.

So, third time lucky. The bell goes as he enters. Maggie had left him right after their trip to El Teide, saying in her usual vague way that she'd 'met some girls'. He had no idea where. 'Up the volcano?' he'd probed. 'Up yours,' she'd replied, sounding suddenly determined. Then she'd picked up her travelling bag and walked out. Not to worry, though. Knowing her, she'll be back before long, apologetic and tearful as always, desperate to show him her love.

He smiles to himself as he steps from the shop, the envelope with the pictures safely in his hands. It's sizzling outside. Siesta time. He'll have a Volcán beer in the *taberna* across the street and get started on the El Teide piece.

But the photos are all wrong. Not his, definitely not. A security guy in mirrored shades. A family, heads lined up like chickens on a perch with no background except sky. What the hell? A fake redhead, eyebrows like curtain rails; at least there are some rocks at her feet. A whole bloody gang of weirdo kids with nightmare dye jobs, paint-box faces and too much metalwork. From the front, from behind, from the side. That weaselly shopkeeper will get an earful, fucking with his customers' pictures! Close-ups now. A snub nose with several diamond studs. A belly ring. Some guy's safety-pinned mouth. Another's arse as he bends down.

What the fuck is all this?

No volcano, goddammit! No lava! No smoke holes!

At the very end two action shots: Maggie in both, grinning and giving him the V-sign.

Diessenhofen Bridge

Leon slumped into the nearest seat in the function suite. The eightieth-birthday concert for his cousin Anna had already begun – some ensemble he'd never heard of. The violinist and the cellist looked in danger of dislocating their shoulders, and the pianist kept tossing his head like a prophet in ecstasy. Leon cringed at their histrionics.

His shirt felt damp after the heat outside. His tie hung like a cut-off noose. He gave it a few half-hearted tugs, ignoring Céline's stare. His niece had no right to judge him, she of all people! He glanced around the rest of the audience, mostly relatives several decades younger than himself. To his left sat Katja. Not his favourite, to be honest: too thin and with a brusqueness that only seemed to emphasise the Gothic flourish of her nose. He'd often wondered why Marcel had married her; Marcel could have had anyone, surely.

Leon hadn't wanted to attend Cousin Anna's birthday party. He didn't fit in, never had. But Céline had needled him into coming. *No sense of family*, what a cheek! His niece knew perfectly well that as a teacher he had always upheld family values. 'The state,' he used to tell her, 'would collapse if everyone behaved with your kind of irresponsibility. Families are the backbone of society.' Yes, this had been his motto all his professional life. Céline being Céline, of course, had simply laughed in his face, taunting him with a 'You try it some time, Uncle!'

The Mozart piece was approaching its climax and Leon wiped his brow with a handkerchief. There was a *föhn* wind again and the air sultry beyond relief. Through the wide-open French windows the Alps seemed etched on the sky, almost within reach. For a moment he fancied he could again smell the warm ripeness of the apples in the hotel's small orchard. His palms still felt prickly from pressing against the roughness of its chest-high wall before the concert: the waiter he'd spoken to at lunch, a young man from Greece, had been lying spread-eagled in the grass on the other side, fast asleep.

It occurred to Leon that in recent years he had grown more like Céline, and she more like him. His niece used to hate bourgeois traditions. 'Rules are there to be broken,' she'd say, and blow cigarette smoke at him. But now that her own daughter had produced three children by as many fathers, she seemed to have quietly opted for the rut of accepted behaviour.

The Mozart had finished and everyone started clapping. Leon winced when Katja flashed him one of her toothy smiles. He could feel the red wine scouring his insides. Not that he had drunk much: the Bordeaux clearly wasn't one of the better vintages and he'd left his second glass three-quarters full. Céline and the younger people must have been rather less discerning, judging by the cluster of empties on their table.

Someone touched him on the arm. 'Enjoyed that, Leon? You're the art expert here.' Marcel, his favourite relative and the best-looking, was leaning towards him, clearly proud of having engaged the piano trio for his mother's birthday.

Feeling flattered, Leon nodded. 'A vigorous interpretation, yes. Full of passion and no holds barred.' Another nod, then a frown for gravitas. 'Thank you so much for the treat, Marcel.'

He wasn't going to mention the wrong notes in the middle movement, or the violinist's slurry ornamentation. Marcel wouldn't have heard them anyway. He was a furniture dealer who bought books by the metre for the shelf units he sold, and chose pictures to go with the sofas and curtain fabrics on display. And yet Leon admired him. He still owned a black and white studio photograph of Marcel as a twenty-year-old, which Cousin Anna had given him in a moment of motherly pride.

After the concert Leon complimented his cousin on her youthful appearance and thanked her for inviting him. Unfortunately he'd have to leave soon to catch his train. Céline would be going with him, to make sure he was okay. To himself he added, Not that I really need a nursemaid. Least of all my niece.

'Oh yes, lovely little Céline,' Anna murmured, with a pointed glance to where Katja was standing, face in profile, laughing and gesticulating. Leon knew she had always hoped for Céline and Marcel to get together. Wishful thinking if ever there was!

'Anyway,' he said to change the subject, 'that was a very enjoyable birthday party, Anna. It'll be my turn before long.'

His cousin patted his hand absent-mindedly, brushing against the red garnet ring on his little finger. Then she seemed to pull herself together and asked, 'Where will you be this Christmas? You're welcome to –'

'Greece,' Leon interrupted, naming the first place that suggested itself – a family Christmas was the last thing he wanted. Year after year Anna would send him parcels of home-made Christmas cookies, glazed or sugar-dusted shapes of angels, stars, birds and hearts, which he'd consign to the dustbin on returning home from some exotic holiday, weeks later. 'You're very kind,' he said now. 'Thank you.' He smoothed down his tie and leant closer for a farewell kiss. Her complexion had that peculiar, peach-skin ruddiness he'd only ever observed in old women who had lost their husbands and found a new lease of life.

A few minutes later Céline minced up on her high-heeled sandals. The top of her head nearly reached his shirt collar. Even in her forties she was still rather pretty, Leon had to admit, with her doll's face, her loose saffron hair all the way down to her waist and the wraithlike figure that made most men instinctively bend forward and talk to her in softened voices.

'You used to be such a stickler for punctuality, Uncle. What made you late for the concert?' She ran a hand through her hair and the broad silver torque on her wrist gave an accusing glint.

Leon shrugged and smiled down into her eyes, cornflower blue like his brother's, dead for more than twenty years. Céline didn't smile back. She swung her head round sharply, her excessive hair flicking at him, and stalked off towards a group of younger relatives whom Leon had no desire to meet.

'Please, Céline, we'll have to go shortly,' he called after her, trying not to sound too pleading. Then he went and stood on the balcony outside the French windows – the panorama of the Alps was magnificent, as was the sight of the waiter still lying asleep in the apple orchard.

Slowly, they teetered and ambled through the noise of Zurich central station. Leon was glad his hearing had blunted slightly with age, which made the incessant shrieks of train brakes, the booming loudspeakers and the high-pitched squeals of the motorised luggage carts more bearable. The whole place offended his aesthetic sensibilities: the monstrous steel struts in the main hall, the conspicuously large clock suspended from the glass roof like a reminder of human transitoriness, and the herd of life-sized wooden cows grazing on the concrete, one striped white and chocolate brown, another decorated with huge, painted-on gentians, a third sporting big silvery blobs like five-franc coins. His thin lips moved silently to form the word 'abomination'.

'So you enjoyed yourself, Uncle?' Céline was looking up at him.

Leon composed himself, then said, 'Oh yes, very civilised. Good food, pleasant company.' It was muggy under the station's glass roof, nothing like the freshness he'd felt near the apple orchard, and he passed a hand over his forehead. 'The music was a nice surprise too, considering.'

His niece blinked innocently, 'Considering what?' He could tell she was resentful at having to escort him back before the party broke up.

'Good God, Céline! You know how much I like Marcel.' He loosened his tie to ease his breathing; the *föhn* weather was getting to him. 'But classical music just isn't his line, is it?'

'Trust you, Uncle, to always find a fly in the ointment.' She pouted, then laughed recklessly and shook out her too-long hair.

Leon remained silent. He was shocked at her flippancy. Humiliated. And acknowledged with a pang that he had misjudged her. She hadn't changed. Not one bit.

When he looked up again, he saw a group of skinheads

approaching. The starkness of their features attracted and repelled him in almost equal measure, and filled him with dread. Trying not to gaze too obtrusively, he pretended to study the departures board behind them. He needn't have bothered. He was thin air. They were all ogling Céline.

Doubly annoyed, Leon glared until he caught the eye of the tallest one, a fellow in his late twenties with razor-sharp cheekbones, a flaccid mouth and a cheetah tattoo below his left ear. The skinhead smiled and spread his hands in what Leon took for a gesture of surrender, then said something that made the others guffaw and press closer to form a wall. Now, still smiling at Leon, Cheetah Man stepped forward and picked up a strand of Céline's hair. His friends clicked their tongues approvingly. Céline didn't budge, simply stood looking down at her feet.

Leon managed to say, 'Now listen, you,' in a quavering old man's voice that was immediately drowned out by the loudspeakers. Then he backed away from the wall of male bodies. Where were the security guards? The police officers patrolling the station? He beckoned to several passers-by: a woman with a rucksack, a young couple, a family, another family … But they all gave the skinheads a wide berth. Leon suddenly felt each year of his life pulling and tugging at him, dragging him to the ground.

Just when he thought he couldn't hold out any longer and would have to sit down, Céline spoke. 'Excuse me,' she said briskly. Then, with a flick of the wrist that made her silver torque flash, she lifted her hair free, grabbed him by the elbow and led the way straight into the wall. And the wall parted as Cheetah Man and his friends turned to stare in silence.

Leon felt terrible. Here had been his chance to protect his niece and he had failed – failed abysmally.

'I'm sorry, Céline. So sorry.'

One of the luggage carts whizzed past, its trailers piled high with suitcases.

Céline glanced up at him and smiled. 'It's not your fault, Uncle. There was nothing you could do.' Her face was as round and pretty as ever, showing no sign that she'd just won a battle of wills. Except perhaps for her eyes. They were darker, and fiercely soft.

'But he was rather good-looking, wasn't he?'

Leon knew whom she meant and didn't answer.

His niece slipped her arm through his. As they carried on walking, her hair floated behind them like a flag of victory.

They found an empty non-smoking compartment in one of the old express carriages that made up the rear of their train. Before Leon could stop her, Céline had slid the door shut, drawn the corridor curtains and pulled the blind down over the half-open window.

'Why not leave the door ajar?' he protested. They were still stationary, probably waiting for a connection, and the air in the *coupé* was so sluggish it seemed to trap itself in his lungs.

'It'll be all right once we start moving.' Céline sank into a seat, drooping visibly. She had the damp, squashed look of a flower clutched in a child's hand for too long, and Leon felt obscurely vindicated. He smiled.

She never noticed; her eyes had closed and her head was lolling to one side. Leon peered out to check on the skinheads, but his view was abruptly cut off by the arrival of a new train. All he could see now was the sausage-and-burger bar further along the platform, with its motley clientele of drunks, dropouts and commuters crowded round the high tables. Through the black mesh of the blind the scene had the melancholy gayness of a Van Gogh painting without the colours.

Next thing the picture was blotted out by several soldiers with heavy-looking backpacks clattering past the carriage. Leon quickly adjusted his tie, then pushed the blind up a little and indicated the free seats within. His red garnet ring glittered in invitation. Some of the men tipped their berets and glanced at Céline, who was rubbing her neck, eyes wide – like a doll someone had suddenly shaken awake.

'What did you have to do that for?' she complained. 'It'll make the place even hotter. Stickier.' To demonstrate how uncomfortable she was, she picked ineffectually at her black dress, whose silky material clung to her chest and thighs in damp ruffles.

'They'd have come in here anyway,' Leon retorted, smoothing the edge in his voice with a false chuckle. 'And I prefer to be welcoming.'

He was in charge again. Still an old man, of course, but a force to be reckoned with. Sitting down for a while had restored him to himself. He gazed at Céline with a tight-lipped smile, then shrugged, irritation mixed with disappointment, the way he used to when he took her to the museum as a child – a twice-monthly occurrence to educate her beyond mere school level – and she'd baulk at some exhibit or other. He still remembered explaining to her the workings of the iron maiden. How on being shut, the various spikes in its door would pierce the eyes and heart of the victim within. By then, of course, his niece was sixteen and no longer a child. Quite ready to be confronted with the horrors of mankind.

Shouts and heavy boots were sounding in the corridor.

Then a soldier stood in the door, smiling. 'Are these seats free, please?'

'Oh, yes.' Leon nodded. Céline waved a languid hand and crossed her legs.

Leon watched as the men hoisted their backpacks into the luggage racks. There were three of them. Burly specimens. Officers, by the look of their epaulettes. The youngest, with a flat pumpkin face, settled down in the seat by the sliding door, stretched out his legs and yawned from ear to ear. 'Sorry, busy weekend,' he muttered, half asleep already. His companions grinned and Leon saw the man opposite him wink.

The train had pulled out of the station and the blind was flapping feebly, creating the faintest breath of wind.

The officer next to Leon turned his head and said conversationally, 'No AC in these old carriages.'

Leon, who didn't understand the phrase 'AC', mumbled something.

Céline gave one of her light-hearted giggles: 'Well, how about the army installing it on humanitarian grounds?'

The two officers laughed.

Leon cleared his throat. This was his chance. 'Actually, when I was in the army we were engaged in quite a lot of civil work. *After* the war, that was.'

The two officers nodded politely and said nothing.

Leon hoped Céline wouldn't point out that he had also served *during* the war. Had been a private in a militia unit dispatched to secure the Rhine border, and ended up witnessing Diessenhofen Bridge being bombed into flames.

For a moment Leon closed his eyes. He was tired, yet strangely electrified by the proximity of the officer beside him. He'd inspected the man's hands. Not a worker's hands, quite definitely. Fine-skinned and covered in golden hairs, with long, strong fingers and neat nails. When the officer had fumbled for a paper handkerchief in his trouser pocket, the touch of his elbow had felt like a nudge.

There was a jolt and Leon realised he must have dropped off. His neighbour was now leaning forward, perched almost on the edge of his seat, and talking with Céline. Discussing action thrillers. The officer next to her was wearing headphones and tapping his foot, a rather sheepish expression on his face.

As soon as the train began to slow for their destination, Leon stood up. His neighbour responded by reaching for his uniform jacket and bringing out pen and paper. Leon tried in vain to get a squint at the note before it was passed to his niece.

'Just ring me if you fancy meeting for a drink.'

'Thanks.' Céline smiled a dopey smile. 'I might do that.'

Leon managed a terse goodbye all round.

Headphones blinked and Pumpkin Face drowsily moved his legs out of the way.

The train stopped. Leon glanced back to see whether Céline

was following – and caught the officer kissing her adieu. He could barely contain himself, stumbled down the corridor and out on to the platform, ignoring Céline who had come up behind him and was extending an arm for support.

Once they were out of earshot, he exploded, 'Really, Céline! You didn't even know him! It's disgraceful!'

Her blue eyes suddenly froze. 'You'd better be quiet now, Uncle.' Her voice, too, was icy. 'Don't think I didn't notice. You could hardly keep your hands off him. What if he'd given *you* his mobile number? Would you have flung it back in his face?'

Leon avoided her eyes. So these were the thanks you got for looking after your own, for cultivating their sensibilities to appreciate the beauties of this world. Classical music. Paintings by the old masters. Frescos restored to their original glory.

He walked on, feeling a little shaky. Shaky and tired, and old. The *föhn* heat had finally beaten him. The *föhn*, that was all.

Heat

It was half past ten and still hot when the Müllers got home, an insubordinate heat that kept slithering and licking along the skin. A nearly full moon quivered through the foliage of the apple tree, its fruit black and flat as cardboard.

Nicole's sandals gave a soft clack-and-slap on the drive as she crossed to the flower border while Rolf finished precision-parking the car in the garage. Bending over the roses, she felt a brief, unpleasant lurch in her belly. Doubtless the effects of too much wine, drunk to wash down Hannah Amati's crackle-dry *saltimbocca* and the pappiness of her saffron risotto. Marco had been a most attentive host, refilling their glasses the way he played tennis, always in the right place at the right time. Marco, with his badly-shaven jaw and the pierced nipple... She would have to let him know, and soon. The thought caused another lurch. Surely the foetus was too tiny to start slopping about yet? One of the roses had come to rest against the hollow of her throat, its petals cool and waxy, like the lightest of caresses. Her own breath seemed to be wafted back to her, clotted now with scent. For a moment she remained in the same position, half-leaning forward, ignoring the footsteps approaching her.

'Communing with your flowers, Nicole?' Husband Rolf put a hand on her shoulder. When he removed it, the silk strap of her dress clung limply to her skin.

She straightened up and smiled at him. 'They smell their love-liest at night,' she said, aware that their perfume had a sickly-sweet edge, just short of decay. 'Be with you in a minute. You go on in.'

'I could help you with the watering. To speed matters up.' Rolf sounded hopeful. Eager for her to follow him into the house, up the stairs and along the corridor to their bedroom, her naked toes brushing against the mossy sensuousness of the oriental rugs. He always wanted to make love to her after they'd been out together and other men had looked at her – in his words – 'with lust in their eyes'.

This time Nicole's smile was tight. 'Thanks, darling, but I'm happy to do it myself.' She paused, wondering vaguely what she meant and how he'd take it. She must have had more wine than she'd realised. 'I won't be long, I promise.'

Rolf had already turned and was heading off towards the house. Sensing his disappointment, she went after him and quickly kissed the damp folds of his neck. 'Love you,' she whispered, slipping away without waiting to hear his reply.

The roses, yellow, salmon pink and blood red by day, were tinged grey in the moonlight. In the grass, the cicadas were shrieking for water. Like sinners craving salvation, it occurred to Nicole, though she wasn't exactly religious. Maybe this was another effect of an evening spent with Hannah, who had become rather churchy over the last year.

It hadn't rained in more than a fortnight. Except for the occasional flashes of sheet lightning that electrified the air and set the nerves jangling, the thunderstorms had held off, bypassing the town either south of the river with its litter of sandbanks, bone-white rocks and sluggish current, or further north beyond the hilly patchwork of vineyards, parched and small and shrinking in the heat.

A week later there had still been no rain. When Nicole woke that Sunday morning, she'd been dreaming of the sky melting above her, dripping fire on her feet. But it was only the sun; it had laid bars across her ankles like branding irons. The bedroom felt stifling despite the open window and balcony door. Even the foamy chiffon curtains hung lifeless. The space beside her was empty, and she slid her body into a diagonal. This was one of the reasons why she enjoyed Sundays. Rolf seemed to be getting up earlier and earlier; he no longer bothered to disturb her in her sleep, was drawn like a worshipper to the stables – and to Saracen, his seven-year-old stallion.

'My wife has her flowers and I have Saracen – flora and fauna, the perfect couple!' he was fond of joking in company, punctuating his words with a few histrionic coughs and a flourish of his gold signet ring, and making Nicole cringe. Rolf insisted on this absurd idea of her as a green-fingered, out-in-all-weathers gardener. He'd probably prefer her living like an elf inside the flower of a bluebell, the acme of femininity. Now, glancing over at his bedside table, she could see the signet ring, a squat, dull gleam against the plastic casing of the telephone. He never wore it while out riding and she wished for a moment that one of the magpies from the garden would swoop in and snatch it away in its beak.

Rolf didn't usually arrive back before mid-afternoon, which left her ample time for a long lie-in with Schubert, Dvořák and Vivaldi or, if she felt wicked enough, with Lee 'Scratch' Perry, Khaled and Goldfrapp. And there was always a pile of new books at her elbow, novels mostly, and the odd thriller. Perhaps, she mused, reading was really her first love.

Today, though, she had other things on her mind. The sheets tore loose as she launched herself out of bed. The sudden movement created a stir among the curtains, and they swayed jerkily to and fro, like people pulled into gossipy knots.

Breakfast over, she changed into a flowing champagne-coloured dress with gold belt and matching sandals, painted her lips vermilion, and locked the front door behind her. The sunlight flicking off the granite steps glittered maliciously. For the hundredth time now Nicole vowed she must learn to drive. How ridiculous, in this day and age, not to be able to do without a chauffeur! Briefly, as she put on her sunglasses, she considered and dismissed the option of cycling. Rolf had presented her with a mountain bike three Christmases ago, so she could go pedal-trampling alongside him and Saracen through the woods and flatlands by the river. A happy family outing doomed never to happen. God, so much was her fault! But she refused to take all the blame.

She stopped by the flower border. The roses needed pruning, and deadheading. It seemed to her that the blood reds in particular had lost their former brilliance.

Marco, of course, had immediately accused her of irresponsibility when she'd given him the bad news last Monday. And yes, it was true, she'd been pretty haphazard about monitoring her periods.

'Are you crazy?' he'd exclaimed into the muted café clatter of gâteau forks and coffee spoons. 'It's impossible!' Then, noticing the disapproving stares around him, he'd lowered his voice to a peevish whisper: 'I trusted you, Nicole. You said it was all right, you did. Why couldn't you have found out sooner, for chrissake?'

Under the tablecloth, his fingers had slipped off her thigh. She'd giggled, near-hysterical, to pretend he'd just told her a funny story. Meanwhile he sat gazing into his cup like a fortune-teller who'd run out of future.

She hadn't heard from him all week. So now she was going to see him. Nicole forced herself upright, away from the roses and their tainted smell. Marco had offered to pay for everything, if necessary even a trip abroad, where the procedure was legal. 'At all costs, Nicole, get rid of it, I'm begging you,' he'd said. 'Hannah would be devastated, and I love my kids.' His eyes had filled with crocodile tears that would have made her laugh had she not felt so much like crying herself, crying and crying, and flooding the whole damn café with her own *real* tears.

But she was over it now. Now she could laugh all she wanted. Instead, she found herself rushing across the lawn, narrowly missing a cluster of velvety black pansies. Some sparrows flew up in a flurry of chatterings. The apples in the tree shone bright gold. She reached up, plucked one at random. It was speckled and sunburnt, and its warmth seemed to pulse against her skin. With a wince she recalled the feel of Marco's smooth, taut body, his hairless chest, the nipple ring's sliding coolness...

She was about to throw the apple away when a squeaky voice cried: 'Can I have it, please?' and one of her neighbours' young grandsons jumped Batman-style from the low wall between the two gardens. He scampered up to her with a big, gap-toothed smile, then was off again, waving the fruit in the air like a trophy.

The church bells began to ring out the end of the service as Nicole went clacking down the cobble-stoned pedestrian precinct. This would have been Hannah's first time as a fully fledged Sunday school teacher, she reflected. The dinner party a week ago had been a bit of a fiasco, to be honest. Marco had been so close, yet so untouchably far. Rolf had kicked up a fuss about wanting to say hello to the children, who'd been put to bed hours earlier and were happily asleep. And Hannah had spent most of the meal recapitulating an Open University lecture she'd attended recently, on Christianity in the New Millennium.

'You're a keen reader, Nicole,' she'd wound up. 'Wouldn't you agree the Bible is the greatest book ever written?' Her tone had been as sugar-sweet as the dessert they'd just finished, a sickly concoction of sponge, cream cheese and chocolate masquerading as tiramisu.

Nicole could tell she was being needled into an argument and made no reply.

Hannah turned to Rolf. 'The Bible's a bestseller,' she insisted. 'No novelist could ever hope to rival those insights into human nature. Not in his wildest dreams.'

While Rolf half-nodded, half-shrugged, laughing in the extra-hearty way that usually preceded the flourish of his signet ring, Nicole had darted a glance at Marco. He'd responded by seizing the pottery bowl on the sideboard next to him and passing it round the table in a clean, slow-motion forehand: 'Have a peach, everyone. From our own espalier.'

They were beautiful white peaches, firm-fleshed, the colour of fresh cream, flushed pink where they'd caught the sun. A special treat, and expected to be appreciated accordingly. Nicole had never been able to eat the downy skin without retching so she picked up one of the fruit knives and started cutting, and peeling.

Which had served to silence Hannah more successfully than any literary debate.

Now, walking along the heat-blistered pavements towards the sports complex, Nicole couldn't help smiling at the memory. A faint smile that hardly curved her mouth.

The inside wall of the restaurant, constructed entirely of plate glass, overlooked the air-conditioned tennis hall like a giant fish tank. All the courts were in use, with quite a few mixed doubles in progress.

Sipping lime juice from a blue-frosted tumbler, Nicole watched Marco on court 3. Weekends were his busiest time, as Hannah had lamented repeatedly in the course of that evening, mumbling about temples, money-lenders and money-making. Until Marco had retaliated: 'But you still take the money, don't you?'

Today he was dressed in the green Dunlop tracksuit whose zip always got stuck three-quarters up, and was coaching a well-tanned brunette. That's how she and Marco had first met. She had fallen for him when he taught her the fast tactical moves at the net, his body only inches from hers, coiled with an energy she suddenly knew she must share – and regret ever after. Nicole clunked her empty tumbler down on the table.

For a lurching moment, the eight courts in the hall seemed to spin out of control and telescope into one as she stared, horror-struck, at the tumult of men, women and children armed with rackets, pounding and slashing at each other ... Nicole gripped the edge of her chair, shut her eyes tight, and held on. When she finally recovered herself, she signalled to the waitress, paid and left.

Marco probably hadn't even seen her. She'd phone him on the mobile during one of his breaks.

'Hey, Nicole, wait! Don't go!'

The side door of the hall had opened and there he was, striding towards her, one arm raised to shield his eyes from the glare.

She stopped, and the day closed in on her, trapped her in

its bell jar of cruel, claustrophobic heat. The champagne dress seemed glued to her belly.

'Listen, sweet, I'm sorry.' Marco took her hand, turned it palm up. The lines in it were glistening with sweat – heart, head, and life – and he slicked his tongue across them gently. After a while he mumbled, 'Sorry for being such a bastard. The least I can do is drive you to that doctor you said would do it, then fetch you home again. And no-one will be any the wiser.'

His brown eyes were smiling down into hers warmly and, Nicole noted, a little selfishly.

'Here's hoping,' she replied and, having scanned the car park behind her, she reached inside his tracksuit to stroke his damp chest and give the nipple ring a tug. 'Let's aim for Friday. I'll need to see the psychiatrist first for a report, though that shouldn't be a problem. He is in cahoots with the doctor, I've heard. Sinks all his money into a private art collection.' She laughed dryly. 'I'll text you tomorrow.' Another tug and she stepped away, miming a kiss.

Mid-morning on Friday and already the sky is simmering towards white-hot. But there's a sense of slackness, an imperceptible trace of dampness in the air. The weatherman has forecast widespread thunderstorms. Somewhere clouds must be piling up, invisibly, like magic see-through castles.

'So the psychiatrist said, "I would advise you to have your child, Frau Müller. If your husband is unaware of the situation, why tell him?" Can you believe this, Marco? And the man calls himself a professional!'

Marco's eyes are on the motorway. 'Greedy quack, trying to save his ass.'

'So I said: "Thanks a lot, Mr Psychiatrist. Once immoral, always immoral, is that it? But I haven't come here to ask your opinion. As it happens, my husband is sterile. Yes, sterile! Now if you'd kindly write that report for the sum agreed?" And I pointedly stared at the only picture on the wall: a Chagall. I was out of there in minutes, report and all.'

Marco grins over at her. 'That's my girl.'

Outside the doctor's surgery they hug, then grow quiet. Marco's gaze keeps flitting to her belly – until she can't bear it any longer. She lifts her dress and grasps his hand, presses it down hard on her naked flesh, demanding in a near-whimper, 'Say goodbye.'

He kisses her on the mouth. 'Be well again, Nicole. I don't want to lose you.'

'There's no reason you should,' she answers. Because of course she'll be back with Marco, afterwards. Rolf need never know about this. Never. And suddenly Nicole feels overwhelmed with gratitude.

Seven hours later she is home once more, and glad to be alive. To celebrate, she sits out on the bedroom balcony with a tinkling glass of orange juice, ice cubes, and the merest shot of vodka. The weather will be breaking soon, she can tell. Behind the vineyards, the magic-castle clouds are dungeon-dark, as if transformed by evil sorcerers. And there's a breeze now, a faint shush against her face. For a moment Nicole is seized by a feeling of utter unreality. Like being in limbo, she thinks to herself, then immediately tries to unthink it. But the phrase won't go away and forms a daisy chain of syllables: *in-lim-bo-in-lim-bo-in-lim-bo ...*

She must have dozed off. The sky has blackened and the cloud-dungeons are glowing purple-yellow. That's when she notices the blood. Her dress and the deckchair are soaked with it; bright red drops are staining the white tiles. There's no pain, just a constant seeping. She pulls off the dress, stuffs it between her legs.

Then, a terry towel wadded into place, she settles herself in bed, very tired now.

She is woken by lightning and whip cracks of thunder. Or was that the garage door crashing shut? It's dark outside, a fake storm-darkness.

'Nicole, where are you?' Rolf's voice.

Rapid footsteps sound on the stairs, along the corridor, muffled by the soft rugs. 'What's wrong, dearest?' He bends over her, kisses her. 'You're as pale as death. Want me to call a doctor?' He smells of horse and the sweetness of hay.

'No, no, I'm fine. Just a rather strong period. I saw the doctor today.' Nicole forces a smile and holds out the prescription she'd been given for an emergency: 'Would you be a darling and get me this from the all-night pharmacy? It's supposed to ease the bleeding.'

Rolf is off like a flash. Then the rain starts flooding down. It runs over the window in streams and torrents. Gusts of wind grab at the curtains bunched near the open balcony door, tossing them about like shackled souls. In the garden, the golden-skinned apples are thrashed to bruises and the roses flayed alive, their petals torn from them and whirled about in a dance of death. Yet the air in the room seems hotter than ever. Ready to ignite, it feels to Nicole.

When Rolf returns his face is stony, but there are deep, wet runnels in it. He tosses the pill packet on the bed and goes to stand on the balcony in the driving rain, his back to Nicole. Fitfully his silhouette is lit up by forked lightning, as though he was its source, or perhaps its target. He is shouting at her. Thunderclaps drown him out. He keeps repeating the same sentences, screaming them into the storm:

'"I'm very sorry, Herr Müller," the pharmacist said as I paid her. "Sorry for what?" I asked.

'I'd no idea, no fucking idea, what that woman was on about. Not until she told me those pills were commonly prescribed for haemorrhages – like after a miscarriage. A miscarriage, Nicole! A CHILD!'

Rolf beats his head against the balcony rail while above him the black skies, lashed with blinding light, roar in fury and in pain.

Nicole lies completely still. She has begun to shiver; it's getting so cold in the room with that balcony door wide open. The bell jar she'd felt herself trapped in these past few weeks has shattered, and now the shards are falling all around her, hailstones as big as a baby's fists.

The Punishment

The days followed each other, always shorter, darker, full of rain and rags of cloud. In the fields, the sheep and cattle stood shivering inside their wet, matted coats. Even the wild geese, having migrated all the way from Siberia to winter down by the village loch, sat huddled in sullen defeat.

Sometimes, when no-one was about, Cathy paid them a visit. She always had a few bits of old bread in her pockets as an alibi. She liked that word, *alibi*. Some of her friends at school had started using it, she didn't know why, perhaps because of what they'd seen on television. Not many people owned one of those, and Cathy's parents certainly didn't. 'Better a warm belly in a warm house than one of those empty boxes,' her mother would say, yanking open the stove door to throw in more coal.

The geese were resting. There were dozens of them, plump, round, silvery shapes whose gabbles were muffled by sleep and feathers. It was easy to sneak up on them.

'Boo! Boo! Boo!' Cathy shrieked and stamped her feet, her arms windmilling her nearly off balance. She laughed out loud as the geese squawked, stiff-necked, then launched themselves at the loch with a clatter, churning the water into a hundred little whirlpools. Some had lifted into the sky, honking, their wings shredding the day's gloom for one brief moment.

Afterwards she picked up some of the feathers they'd shed in fright; they were soft, almost warm, with a pearly greyness that shimmered in her hands. She put them in her skirt pocket, then brought out the crusts of bread and scattered them on the ground: her alibi.

Her parents' house was long and narrow, built in one smooth curve that followed the main street as it sloped from the manse down to Drouthie Neebours and up again towards the school. At the back door Cathy took off her shoes. She still felt bored; the chasing and yelling hadn't helped. It was the middle of another grey Saturday afternoon. Her friend Lorna was ill with chicken pox and her older sister Dorothy had gone into town with some other girls, no doubt to Woolworth's for cheap make-up. Before Dorothy found Cathy's company 'too silly', they would sometimes dab starch on their faces and redden their lips with beetroot, then sit on the sofa in their best clothes, pretending to be ladies, expensively dressed, powdered and lipsticked, travelling on a train.

'A train to bloody nowhere,' Cathy now said out loud, without meaning to.

Her mother looked up from the kitchen table where she was chopping vegetables for a stew. 'Don't swear, Cathy, I keep telling you.' Her voice had an edge to it and Cathy knew in a flash that her father must have gone to Drouthie Neebours again.

'Where's Dad?' she asked innocently.

'He had to do something,' her mother said vaguely, glancing away. Then her knife hacked into a turnip, decapitating it. That was another word Cathy liked, *decapitate*.

The radio was on in the background and a woman was saying: 'Christmas decorations don't have to cost the earth, you know. Get an armful of spruce and holly cuttings, a small can of silver spray, some florist's wire and a good supply of foil-wrapped sweeties – little red chocolate hearts are a winner with children –'

'I'm starving.'

Cathy's mother smiled, 'Go ahead, then. There's a loaf in the cupboard and a new jar of raspberry jam.'

There was always a choice to be made. Either butter or jam – the luxury of both was unthinkable. Except for Cathy's father.

As Cathy ate her slice of bread, which she'd smeared with jam, extra-thick, while her mother's back was turned, she wriggled her toes in time to the accordion music that had replaced the radio lady's voice. They stuck damply to her woollen stockings, and she wondered if she ought to have hidden her shoes instead of leaving them in plain view, clotted with wet, down-speckled earth.

With her left hand she felt for the softness of the goose feathers in her skirt pocket – and imagined them gleaming in the dark.

'I know what you could do,' her mother said once Cathy had cleared away her plate. 'Why don't you light the fire in the sitting room and have a wee read, nice and cosy.' She smiled encouragingly.

Cathy shrugged and stared at the coals in the stove. They seemed to glare back at her, their brightness so intense it hurt her eyes. The stupid feathers weren't enough. Not even their secret gleamings. Nothing could fight that terrible sense of boredom and loneliness that followed her around everywhere, down to the loch, into the house, the kitchen, burrowing right into her head.

Then suddenly she heard her mother add: 'If you promise to be careful, you can have a look at your father's bible.'

Cathy let go of the feathers in her hand. Excitement swept through her, and her heart beat a little faster.

'I promise,' she said and quickly ran off.

Her father had two bibles, but she knew instantly which one her mother meant. Not the unwieldy heirloom with the stained and creaking calfskin and the flyleaf full of names, verses and dates like an ancient tombstone. No, this one fitted snugly into her hands. It was bound in delicately tooled, red Morocco leather that had a musky, exotic smell, and its pages were the colour of ivory, as smooth as silk.

To Cathy this small red bible represented everything she secretly, and hopelessly, aspired to: sophistication, beauty, femininity. Here was a whole cluster of her most treasured words: *femininity*, all soft and contented-sounding, *sophistication*, with its hint of sharpness underneath the finery, and *aspiration* as the key to both.

On the flyleaf it said in her grandmother's elegant handwriting: *'To our son Thomas on his twenty-first birthday. May God be with you always. Your loving parents.'*

Cathy envied her father. How could a man like him, a man who spent his days among broken-down machinery and his evenings wrecking himself with drink, possess something so perfect?

The fire in the sitting room was already laid. Cathy struck a match and watched as the flames attacked the kindling and balls of newspaper, then the logs.

When it was time to sacrifice the feathers, she dropped them one by one, and one by one they flared up, raining tiny sparks as they curled in on themselves with a stench like burning hair. Afterwards she snuggled into the armchair and began stroking and sniffing the red leather, flicking her tongue over one corner experimentally (it tasted sour), fingering the pages while dreaming of cedar wood, milk and honey, of cream made into mountains of sweet butter, of loaves and fish that multiplied to feed thousands, and of water turned into wine.

For the past week she had been pestering her parents to let her take the red bible to Sunday School. To show it to the world, or at least to her friends. 'Only the once; I'll look after it, I swear – cross my heart and hope to die, please, please, please.'

Now, holding it on her lap, drowsy from the heat, she felt there was nothing she wanted more. Tomorrow was Sunday. If necessary, she would beg her parents on her knees.

'Tea's ready, girls!' Her mother's voice came from far away and Cathy stayed where she was, playing with Lorna in a dream meadow of red, blue and yellow flowers, splashing each other with buckets of milk from a stream whose banks were covered in buttered and honeyed slices of bread.

'Hey, wee one, wake up!' Dorothy was shaking her and Cathy could see right up her shouting mouth, beyond the swollen-looking tongue to the dark, fleshy throat at the back.

Cathy scowled, then remembered the red Morocco bible on her lap and crossed her hands over it. But her sister had already snatched it up. She laughed. 'Studying for Sunday School, were you?' She arched her brows like a schoolmistress. Then Cathy realised her sister wasn't trying to be nasty: she was waiting for her to admire her new eyeshadow. 'Nice colour,' Cathy said dutifully, although it reminded her of an owl's wing, all dusky shades of amber and brown.

Their father wasn't home yet, but they sat down at the kitchen table anyway and started to eat.

'Please, Dorothy, wipe that stuff off your eyes, will you?' their mother said. 'You know your father doesn't like you all painted up like a cheap skirt.'

Cathy looked down at her own skirt, bought at Woolworth's last year. It hadn't cost a lot.

'Dad isn't here, Mum; he never is on a Saturday night.' Dorothy had another spoonful of the stew.

'He'll be home any minute now, you know he will.' A pause. 'He said he would. I told him we'd have the rabbit he snared yesterday. He promised me. He promised!' Cathy noticed how her mother's voice had grown louder and shriller as she spoke, and she glanced up from her plate. But her mother had turned away to blow her nose. Dorothy got to her feet, put the radio on, then stealthily rubbed off her eyeshadow with the hem of her cardigan before sitting down again.

While they finished their meal, they listened to the music on the radio in silence: cheerful fiddle tunes that cried out for 'The Dashing White Sergeant', and Cathy tried to fill her heart with them.

They were clearing the table when her mother said, 'Oh, Cathy, you can take the bible to Sunday School tomorrow if you want.'

Cathy could have jumped for joy. Instead she merely whispered, 'Thank you, Mum,' and reached for the tea towel to help Dorothy with the washing up. Good fortune was like goose feathers, easily frayed and blown away by the wind.

Seconds later she heard the stove door open and close. Then there was a hiss and a sizzle and the stench of burning meat. Inside the stove, a host of flames would be leaping up in a wild dance round the rest of the stewed rabbit. Cathy stared at her mother, but she simply picked up the empty coal scuttle as if nothing had happened, and went outside.

'What a bloody waste!' Her sister banged the dishes round the sink, making some of the water slosh over the edge. 'I'd have eaten that. Now, Cathy, get a move on.'

Cathy woke with a start. It was dark and something had crashed to the floor by the back door. She heard her father shout, 'Fucking mess in this fucking house!' then the sound of the back door opening and slamming shut again, then more swearing and his footsteps shuffling down the hall to her parents' bedroom. She put her fingers in her ears, pulled the blanket over her head and tried to picture the small red bible on her bedside table.

Her father didn't get up next morning because he 'needed a rest', as her mother called it. Going off to Sunday School a little later, the red bible safely stowed in her coat pocket, Cathy saw her dirty shoes lying in the garden outside the back door. They were soaked by the rain that must have fallen during the night, and looked as if they'd been given a good kicking. She knew better than to dry them by the kitchen stove and hid them in the shed, glad she was wearing her Sunday shoes.

The Sunday School teacher had a wart stuck between the lashes of her left eye, and her spittle flew far and wide. One time, she'd made Big Joe and some of his friends sit in the front row so they would behave themselves, and they'd opened an umbrella. In her fury she'd spat worse than ever and they'd all ducked behind their bibles.

Cathy was early, and the teacher nowhere in sight. 'Abracadabra!' she cried as soon as she entered the church hall, and out shot her hand with the red bible.

None of the children inside seemed to hear her. They were all crowding round the wrought-iron stove in the middle of the hall. Not for warmth. The boys were having another game of spitting, and betting. The drops would run round the flat, sizzling hot stove lid like mercury, and whoever's spit lasted longest won the bet. Somehow, Sunday School meant spittings, one way or another.

'Abracadabra!' This time Cathy yelled and several of them glanced over at her before turning back to their game. For a moment she stood quite still, gazing down at the words HOLY BIBLE tooled in the beautiful red leather.

Suddenly she found herself rushing forward. She couldn't help it. Something stronger than her forced her on. She shoved past two thin girls from the neighbouring village. Elbowed aside Tommy Four-Eyes. Then slammed into Big Joe.

'Hey,' he said, jostling her, 'clear off, Cathy, I'm warning you.'

She ignored him. Now she was right in front of the stove. She raised the red bible up high. The heat seemed to singe her face. 'See this?' she screamed, her voice breaking, but there was no choice now, no choice. She had finally caught everyone's attention. They were all staring at her.

'Watch!' She half threw, half placed the bible on the stove lid. The bottom side shrivelled up almost at once. And it stank. God, how it stank.

Tommy Four-Eyes pushed back his glasses. 'It's a bible! It's a bible!'

The boys roared, whistled. The girls shrieked.

Then Big Joe's arm sliced past her and swept the smouldering, blackened and blistered remains off the stove. The bible hit the floor with a slap.

'I'll tell Miss Rutherford,' one of the thin girls squeaked.

'Oh no, you won't,' Big Joe and the other boys chorused. 'No-one'll tell her. Or else…'

Cathy sensed they were all looking at her, but she couldn't see them. They had become blurry figures beyond the tears that glazed her eyes and dripped off her cheeks on to the bible at her feet.

Her parents didn't scold her, never said a single word. They didn't beat her. Nothing. Cathy kept waiting for her punishment.

Hoping for it. At night in bed. In the morning on getting up. In the afternoon, returning from school. And every so often, when she least expected it, she would come across the object of her shame, lurking in some cupboard or drawer, displayed on a shelf: one side of it quite intact, still red and beautiful, with the words HOLY BIBLE perfectly legible, the other charred and ugly.

Clearing her parents' house almost fifty years later, Cathy unlocked her mother's bedside cabinet ... and there, next to the old-fashioned jewellery box, was the little red bible. For a moment she hesitated – she could hear Dorothy clattering about in the kitchen – then she picked it up. The scorched cover hadn't been repaired and still seemed to smell faintly of burning. On the flyleaf, beneath her grandmother's copperplate, a new inscription had been added: 'To our daughter Cathy.'

Snow White and the Prince

Like a little girl I've waited and waited for this day. The date is engraved on my heart; no doubt it'll be found there, seared into my flesh, when they open me up after death.

Twenty-seven minutes past four. Dusk has fallen outside, silvering the uncurtained bay window with a sheen of dampness. I switch on the table lamp. My gold watch ticks the seconds away ever more loudly. The Roman numerals blur into each other as I give the glass lid another polish on the sleeve of my blouse. It's my best blouse, reserved for Sundays – for special days.

Twenty-nine minutes past four. Patience, Alice, I tell myself. Five o'clock on a Sunday is a more decent time to telephone almost-strangers; they'll have had their afternoon nap and won't yet be sitting down to supper.

There goes the cat flap, a muffled double-bang that breaks up the sluggishness of waiting.

'Trixie?'

She is a killer, this one, a tiger right down to the stripes, with slitted demon eyes that are hard to outstare. I just hope she hasn't caught a bird again. She's brought home two already this past week. A small sparrow, torn and mute, barely alive, its eyes black with terror until I helped it out of its misery. Then a dead blackbird, an old female with gnarled, twig-like feet and a touch of mould around the base of its beak. It looked so pathetic I found a Cadbury box, lined it with twigs, moss and leaves like a nest, and tucked the sorry creature inside.

Twenty-eight minutes to five. I've always cherished this watch, ever since that day fifty-one years ago when Sean said in his Irish lilt-and-drawl, 'Alice! Surprise, surprise, close your eyes!' and fastened it round my wrist. Sleekly cool the gold had felt on my skin, until Sean kissed me and the metal began to glow with our love; the warmth spread through my body, from my arm into my shoulder and all the way down and everywhere – even now at times I can feel a small ripple of it, as if a trace of that heat was forever trapped in my body's memory.

It had taken us two-and-a-half years to reach this first stage of the courting ritual. The first and last, as things turned out. No ring from him, ever.

A decade later I did get a ring. I 'inherited' a wedding ring (no question of an engagement ring from the man who asked for my hand, though not for my heart). 'Have this as my mother's blessing,' my late husband said, slipping it on my finger. The metal was dulled by drudgery, etched with the tiny, filigree lines that come from too much scouring, washing and cleaning.

I was quick on the uptake. Learnt to patch and mend the already patched and mended curtains of what used to be *her* house. Learnt to beat the rugs and sweep out the cold ash from the hearths just as *she* used to do. Learnt to air the sewn-up old overcoat which protected the mattress from the springs of the double bed that used to be *hers*. The three children, at least, were mine. I bought them new beds, new curtains and new rugs for their rooms. Sometimes I pictured my dead mother-in-law super-vising me from the spirit world, and I stuck out my tongue at her.

'Trixie, puss, puss.' No bird today, thank God. 'Here, jump on up. That's better, isn't it? Cosier for both of us.'

We had seemed an item, Sean and I. The architect-to-be and the hairdresser. Both sculptors of sorts, we'd joke. To this day, I can reel off facts and figures about Georgian, Victorian or Edwardian buildings. And I can still feel the thick, silky texture of Sean's dark brown hair between my fingers as I scissor-snipped it into shape. Near-white it'll be by now.

I hoped he would never graduate. Never leave. I'd grown to hate the long summer holidays he spent away from me, in Ireland. Hated the parting kisses at Caley Station that made me cry and take refuge in St Cuthbert's Cemetery, flinging myself down on De Quincey's grave.

But Sean's finals did come. And his graduation. On the night before his return to Belfast I desperately clung to him in the doorway of my lodgings, then watched him walk away towards Marchmont. When he crossed the street, it felt like a stab in the heart. I knew in a flash that this was the beginning of the end – and that he would always, always be my love.

'Poor you, Trixie. Not many eligible toms in the neighbour-hood, are there?'

For the next year or so Sean and I carried on visiting each other across the Irish Sea. He'd doss down on some architect friend's floor here in town – we were so damnably proper! – and I'd stay with his family.

Then his sister got engaged. His mother took me aside to tell me the good news. 'Isn't Shonagh's engagement ring lovely, Alice?' she asked with a big smile. 'And only six months since the gold watch!' Perhaps it was just the proud mother speaking. Perhaps. But she must have been aware that I hadn't got beyond the gold watch in seventeen months.

I'd been annoyed for ages that Sean was continually surrounded by his friends when I was in Belfast. They stuck to him like limpets. Sought him out at the house, showed up in pubs, joined us for walks, dances, the pictures. It was always him and his friends – and me. Quite unlike our closeness in Edinburgh.

'What do you mean, "never alone"?' Sean said, his voice suddenly hard and liltless. 'They're my friends! I've known them all my life.'

'I'm your friend, too. Your best friend, I hope.'

'That's different. You're my *girl*. They're my *friends*.'

'But surely you can get them to back off a bit while I'm here? For a day or two?'

'Don't you want my friends?'

'Don't you want me?'

Back in Edinburgh I became sick. My heart felt bruised, and I had to take time off work. I kept wondering what was wrong with me. Was I simply an uncompromising, selfish bitch? An idealist? Or a naive, romantic lassie? Probably a mixture of all three – and I still am, I suppose. Surely, I told myself, some people feel more deeply, more intensely, than others? Because I loved Sean to the exclusion of everyone else, I expected the same of him. I'd drawn a magic circle around us, and God forbid if anyone tried to trespass. I reread the poems of Rupert Brooke, a gift from my friend Kitty, and let myself sink into their melancholy rhythms of lost love.

In the end I sent Sean a letter. I tried to explain my feelings. Tried to explain without sounding all jealous and melodramatic. I was twenty-six years old and I knew I'd passed on my great – my only – love.

Sean wrote back by return. Pleaded. Asked why? What had he done? Didn't I want to share my life with him?

Yes, of course I wanted to share my life with him, for ever and ever! But I couldn't – wouldn't – share *him*.

Five months after we had finished I received a small package. Inside was the narrow leather box with my grandfather's amber and wrought-silver cigarette holder that I'd given to Sean. Again he begged me to reconsider.

I've reconsidered all my life...

Twenty more minutes. Time has slowed to a snail's pace. I wish I could curl up like you, Trixie, and purr away the minutes in happy oblivion. My feet, gnarled and brittle as the dead black-bird's, are too unsteady now for a good long hike to tire out body and soul.

It must have been the summer after Sean and I split up, one of those luscious, sultry Sundays when people went to church for coolness, not worship. But I could think of a better place to escape the heat. I skipped the service and – none of my friends being around for company – took the train out to Roslin all by myself.

My mother was from Rosewell and her best friend lived in one of the houses in the Glen, long before it became the Country Park. I used to run wild with the Glen children. We played hide-and-seek in the woods, splashed about in the North Esk with its gungy, coloured foam from the carpet factory. We raced up and down the steps of Jacob's Ladder, sneaked along the fence of the gunpowder mill to watch the horses pull their dangerous loads, hands clapped to our ears in case there was an explosion. Or we explored the gorge and Wallace's Cave and dared each other to go near the castle at dusk. But hope as I might, I never once met the Black Knight on horseback, never once saw the White Lady, and never once heard the baying of the Phantom Hound.

The Glen echoed with voices on that hot, bright Sunday afternoon. Picnic rugs and folding chairs dotted the river banks; some people were enjoying a late lunch, others sat chatting and smoking; children chased by dogs were paddling in the water or throwing balls.

The shade of the trees felt refreshing as I strolled past families and past couples with happy, shining faces. I chose the paths at random, up and down, left and right, zigzagging – keeping my favourite spot, the castle, for last.

When I finally stood on the giant stone bridge in the glittering sunlight, the sheer drop down into the Glen took my breath away, yet again. I raised my arms in greeting – and froze. The glass lid of my treasured gold watch, where was it? I almost cried out. Compulsively checked and re-checked the rolled-up sleeves of my blouse, inside my handbag, under the waistband of my skirt. Sweating now, I retraced my steps along the cobbles of the bridge. The trees started to close in on me, forming malevolent, endlessly winding tunnels of darkness, penetrated only here and there by dusty shivers of light. I strained my eyes, scanned the ground, scanned roots that had turned into sinuous arms and grasping hands, scanned mouldering leaves, the soil beneath giant horse-tails and ferns. Nothing. Not a glint. Above me in the trees I could hear the swish of wings, heavy, portentous. A woodpecker drilled mechanically. There were rustles in the undergrowth. Shouts rang out from the river, and laughter. Barks.

It was hopeless, of course. Like trying to find a needle in a haystack. The lid could have fallen off anywhere. It might have dropped into the water from the footbridge. Or perhaps someone had picked it up and kept it for luck – there were enough people about, after all. Not that I had the courage to accost any of them.

Just then I noticed a middle-aged couple coming towards me, tall, well-dressed, arm-in-arm. The woman was wearing a lovely, ivory-coloured frock and she had a pale, genteel face with silvery curls. On an impulse, I decided to speak to her.

She pre-empted me with a 'Can we help you?'

Her kindliness nearly made me burst into tears and I stuttered out my story. She listened patiently, then pointed to the ground. 'There,' she said with a smile. 'Look, it's right there, next to your shoe.'

So it was. The small glass disk was lying at my feet, and it didn't have a single scratch.

I stared up at the woman. She was still smiling, but her eyes seemed to flicker, very briefly.

How I got home that day I can't remember; I might have flown for all I know. It was as though, for a fleeting moment, I'd been allowed a glimpse of the invisible pattern that governs our lives.

One evening three years later I came out of the hairdressing salon in George Street where I worked and set off towards South Charlotte Street as usual when, up ahead, standing deep in conversation, I saw Sean.

Surely it couldn't be? Surely not? His tell-tale round shoulders were stooping now, no doubt from bending over the drawing board too much. I recognised the other man too: George Kerr, one of his friends. I was paralysed by a sense of déjà vu. As if there was a film stored inside me, ready to roll. Presently, I was certain, Sean would spot me and come rushing up, laughing, shouting, 'Alice! Hey, Alice!' I grabbed hold of the window ledge behind me, feeling giddy all of a sudden.

Something was wrong with the film. Or perhaps it was the wrong film. Because Sean didn't turn round, didn't spot me. He walked off. And I followed him blindly, like a dog. Just as I summoned up the courage to go up to him, he was joined by a woman who had emerged from a shop. They kissed, crossed the street and together disappeared inside the Roxburghe Hotel.

Instead of trundling home by tram, I ran. Ran all the way up Lothian Road and through the Meadows to my lodgings. Ran as fast as I could so my heart would break, at last.

But some hearts take a lot of breaking.

Once inside, I poured myself a large G & T, then rang Kitty, who used to know Sean well. Would she mind telephoning the Roxburghe and speak to him, for old times' sake?

She called me back two and a half G & Ts later. The receptionist had said Mr O'Connor wasn't in and Kitty had hazarded: 'What about Mrs O'Connor?' Mrs O'Connor was out too. Kitty had left her number for Mr O'Connor.

Sean was married. MARRIED! To someone else.

I let myself drop into the fusty old armchair by the telephone and started crying.

'Cheer up, Alice, there are plenty more fish in the sea. Thousands and thousands.'

I merely snuffled.

Kitty told me the rest. Sean had rung her back and, after they'd talked about this and that – life in Belfast and Edinburgh, their respective careers (Kitty was a nurse at the Sick Children's Hospital), how he'd met his wife (she'd replaced him as architect at Stormont when he set up his own business) – he had finally brought the conversation round to me, asking was I married.

'Oh, no,' she'd replied, 'not Alice. She has never looked at another man.'

There'd been a long silence. Then, like a little boy stamping his foot, Sean had blurted out, 'But my parents saw her at the Braemar Highland Games – with her husband, they said. They were positive it was her.'

I gasped and interrupted Kitty: 'I haven't been to those games in my life, I swear to God!'

'Don't worry, Alice, that's exactly what I told Sean. He went dead quiet after that.'

At noon next day I was in the middle of doing a blue rinse for one of the elderly Turtle-Necks (as we used to call them) when the salon bell dinged. The other hairdresser and the apprentice were out at lunch so I tugged open the cubicle curtain –

And there he was. Leaning against the counter by the door.

The salon bell kept dinging in my ears as I stared at him, unable to move. Sean. *My* Sean. Seconds later he'd dashed up to me and we embraced.

We kissed …

Until the old lady began to complain about the blue rinse trickling down her face. As I got busy cleaning her up, Sean hovered by my side, touching my arm every so often. 'Can't you spare ten minutes, Alice? Please?' I shook my head, indicating Turtle-Neck, whose hair dye needed rinsed off. (I couldn't risk the scant remainder of her locks falling out, could I? Yet, for one mad moment, I caught myself thinking, 'Dammit, she can wear a wig!')

Sean only had another quarter hour before the conference on architecture resumed. 'I wish I wasn't leaving tomorrow morning,' he said sadly as we kissed goodbye. 'I'll be in Edinburgh again in a few months' time and look you up then, I promise.'

That was forty-six years ago.

But now the waiting is over. It is five o'clock. Yes, Trixie, no use pretending surprise. I can feel my body quivering, on the brink of one last adventure. Easy to picture that poor blackbird of yours, jerkily poised on the grass, its mouldy beak probing the earth – while you lurk unseen …

I've already checked with international directory enquiries (did that this morning, like an impatient young thing). Spelled his name, spelled Belfast (for good measure) and, lo and behold, his number was revealed to me, digit by digit. Not that this guarantees he is still alive. But I am too old now not to take risks.

'Hello?' A woman's voice, rather frail.

I ask all the more firmly, 'Could I speak to Sean O'Connor, please?'

When she inquires who should she say, I nearly weep with

relief.

'Just say someone from Edinburgh,' I reply, almost airily.

He gives his name in the familiar lilt-and-drawl, and hearing it after all these years cuts my heart, yet again.

I want to shout, It's Alice! *Your* Alice! Instead I say, 'This is someone from Edinburgh.'

'From Edinburgh?' He sounds puzzled and I imagine him frowning. Even as a student he had a vertical line between his eyes; by now it will be a furrow.

How could he have forgotten me? How could Edinburgh not mean the one and only thing to him? How could he have forgotten my voice? How?

In the end I have to tell him. 'It's Alice,' I say, hurt and crest-fallen. Then I add, 'Chalmers'. Because I couldn't bear him not recalling me at all; I know I'd start blubbering and never stop.

'Ah, Alice!' A spark of recognition now, thank God. 'How are you?' But there is something in his tone that warns me to tread softly. He, at least, has had a good marriage, it seems. I wish him many happy returns on his seventy-fifth birthday.

'You remembered after all this time?'

'Of course.' *And I've been waiting – waiting and hoping silly little-girl hopes.*

For a while we talk about nothing very much. I mention that I've been widowed for almost twenty years, mention the shop, the children, the grandchildren, the cat. Soon, we hang up.

'What else is there to say, eh, Trixie? I'm so glad you are a fighter and a killer. You will survive.'

The winter dark has crept up on me unawares. The windowpanes are tarred black now, with the table lamp a feeble glow in the far left corner. Trixie stretches, yawns and leaps to the floor, where she slides and squirms in and out of my legs, doing figures of eight accompanied by miaows. Then she jumps up on my lap again, begins to paw at my hands, her claws out for more effect. A cunning little beast. If only I'd been born a cat.

'I'm coming,' I say wearily and for a moment she gazes at me with her big, slitted demon eyes. I force myself to my feet. I feel wobbly all of a sudden. 'Yes, yes, Trixie, I'm coming.'

I leave her seven dishes heaped high with the contents of seven tins, leave her seven bowls filled to the rim with fresh water. As if she were all the seven dwarfs rolled into one. And I Snow White. I chuckle. I've been saving up my sleeping pills.

Then I look at my gold watch. It has stopped.

The pattern, I know, is complete.

I might just allow myself a last few slices of apple. Not that there is much hope of me choking on them. And even if I did, my prince will never arrive. Will never ride across the seven hills. Never brave the stormy seas.

Smell the Roses

The flat smelled sweet the day I invited Michael's family. Flowers everywhere. I can't do without them at the best of times, the bouquets of lilies, the sprays of roses and babies'-breath, the too-delicate freesias, which bruise so easily. And that Saturday was the worst of times: now Michael was buried, I had decided to tell his family the truth. After all, I'd known them for almost as long as I could remember.

Vasefuls of pastel-hued freesias and roses in different shades of pink and cream stood like phials of perfume on top of the display cabinet, on the coffee table, the bookcases, the bathroom window sill, the pottery workbench down the hall. A single bird of paradise flower leaned waxy-cool against the rim of an old wine bottle in my bedroom. And a blue-enamelled floor vase by the kitchen door held several white oriental lilies, their blooms paper-thin now and curling at the edges, their fragrance moribund: Michael's lilies.

'Better times!' Vera lifted her glass of Chablis and slowly swung it round the coffee table, stirring up the scent of my shell-pink roses. As if she were in charge. As if she herself had seated her mother Isa, brother Roland and sister Karin on my sofa and chairs, had herself personally arranged for the late afternoon sun to spread a blush through the blossoms of the Japanese cherry tree outside the window. Her severe black dress seemed oddly becoming, like that of a proper hostess. Then she smiled, and the image began to crumble. She smiled without really looking at any of us – a kind of sliding smile, like a layer of watery clay that refuses to stay put.

Why couldn't I simply reach out to her, perhaps even whisper some words of sympathy? Was I jealous? She'd always been Michael's favourite, and his death had hit her hard. But Michael had been part of *my* life, too. He and my late father, or the man I used to call my father, had been best friends.

The memory of them both made my eyes cloud over and I quickly bent forward to smell the roses, and calm myself. Then I glanced at Roland on the sofa opposite. He was Michael's eldest, three years younger than me – and my ally, I hoped.

He ignored me, communing with his wine instead.

Abruptly Vera pushed her chair away and stood smoothing the black dress over her hips with a circular motion that meant business. 'I'll check on Baby, shall I?' she announced.

'Don't you dare,' Karin snapped in sisterly rivalry. 'Baby's fine if she isn't crying, Vera, I've told you before. Just leave her alone.' There was a ray of sunlight on her left cheek, a transient scar glittering from lips to brow bone. She was beautiful, I couldn't help thinking, the most beautiful of us all.

Roland continued to sip his Chablis, his face inscrutable. Ever since they'd arrived in that squat, constipated BMW, he had been acting strange, looking at me askance. Accusingly. But I wasn't to blame for our shared secret. Not that he knew the half of it, of course.

Vera was still hovering by her chair.

'Oh, please stop quarrelling, girls.' Isa's fat, ringed hands fluttered ineffectually in her lap, like two white birds trapped in a cage.

I pretended to inspect my turquoise-painted toenails, wishing suddenly they'd all drive away so I wouldn't have to go through with my confession. I didn't need their approval, did I? In my mind, I pictured the partially modelled boy's head on my work-bench, commissioned for a wedding anniversary, and I felt an unreasonable tenderness towards it.

'Why do you always have to quarrel?' With a sigh of exasperation, Isa sank deeper into the sofa cushions beside Roland.

'Right then, something to eat?' Vera started moving towards the kitchen.

I made to get up too, forcing my feet back into the high-heeled sandals. When I'm by myself, I usually go barefoot. My flat's well-heated all year round – a hothouse home for my hothouse flowers – and I enjoy letting my toes play with the lumps of wet clay as I sit working.

'No help necessary,' Vera said over her shoulder. 'It's stuff from the deli. Won't take a minute.' Then, turning briefly to look at me, she added, 'You can entertain everyone.'

But 'everyone' included *me*, surely? And this was *my* flat. *My* party – even though I'd asked them to bring the food and wine, at my expense, naturally. Exhaustion due to a bout of flu had been my excuse for not attending Michael's funeral the previous week. I couldn't have sat through the prayers and hymns. The tears.

I did Vera's bidding and kicked off my sandals. For a moment I found myself staring at the withered lilies. Two nights before he died, I had gone to see Michael at the hospital, and he'd said to buy them: 'You love flowers, and so do I.' Then he told me about the account he'd set up for me with my local florist's, and that he'd asked Roland to manage it. When I wanted to thank him, he placed his thin, blue-veined hands on mine, saying there was something else – his 'final confession', he called it. In the end we both cried and he asked my forgiveness. I kissed him, more tenderly than ever. Afterwards I bought the lilies. I vowed to keep them for as long as their petals would cling on ...

'Hey, Vera, come here a minute!' Roland was leaning forward.

'What?' Vera stepped from the kitchen, arms folded defensively across her chest.

Roland waved his wineglass at her. 'Just slow down, Sis, okay? You haven't stopped once since I flew up. You're like a ... like a ...' He frowned around the room, his glance skittering disdainfully past me, past the roses and freesias, the display cabinet with my clay busts of popular icons (Monroe, Princess Diana, Madonna, Elvis, Michael Jackson), settling at last on the flower-painted face of the wall clock I'd bought at a car-boot sale. 'Like an overwound clock.' He finished his sentence with a grin. 'Sweet little Karin here will be happy to assist, I'm sure.'

'Why not you?' Karin hissed. Her eyes flashed lightning-blue;

her ivory complexion was mottled. 'You're getting on my nerves, man.'

Roland laughed, then blew her a kiss.

I turned away and saw Vera give him an almost pleading look before she brushed past the lilies to go back into the kitchen. The hem of her dress was dotted with orange pollen stains, and a couple of the worn-out petals drifted to the floor.

Isa shook her head when Roland offered her a refill, pursing her lips in disapproval. Poor Isa. Her body had set in a permanent slump of sadness, from her drooping eyelids to her swollen feet in the heavy lace-ups.

As Roland topped up my glass, some of the wine slopped over my hand and he glared at me. 'Fancy keeping a bunch of dead flowers,' he said loudly. 'You could afford fresh ones, couldn't you?'

'Roland, please.' Isa sounded weary.

'Couldn't you?' he prompted again.

I said nothing.

We all sat in silence and drank.

Why hadn't I waited a few more weeks before inviting them? It was too soon after Michael's death, the pain too raw. And what difference did it make, anyway, whether they knew or not? Whether they suspected things – and the wrong things at that? Michael had been the link between us, the glue that held us all together like the shards of a cracked piece of pottery. Wasn't it enough that *I* knew? I dug my toes into the thick pile of the rug, gulped down the Chablis and gazed into the dusky cherry-tree blossoms outside. From the kitchen came the rustle of cellophane and the clatter of plates and cutlery.

Suddenly, a howl started up in my bedroom. Karin was off like a shot.

Once Baby was safely asleep again, we all filed into the kitchen. My stomach felt tight and I avoided Roland. Vera had laid out a gourmet array of cold meats, smoked salmon, cheeses, salads, rolls and fruit tartlets. Next to the dishes stood several tumblers bunched with bright yellow daffodils.

'How lovely, Vera, thank you!' I touched her on the shoulder.

'You're welcome.' She smiled wryly. 'Not that you're short of flowers.' I flinched, but then her arms went round me in a tight embrace. 'I miss him so much,' she sobbed. 'The best father anyone could ever have.'

I pressed against her. My eyes were watering, magnifying the gleam of the two wedding rings on Isa's left hand as she chose a floury roll from the basket. No-one spoke, the only sounds the clinking of the serving spoons and the dull scrape of the cheese knife on the wooden board.

I restricted myself to a slice of honey-cured turkey and a brown roll, with a strawberry tartlet for afters. 'Still not feeling too good,' I explained.

It had grown dark outside and we'd been eating for a while, balancing the plates on our knees, when Baby broke into renewed howls. Karin put her plate down on the coffee table, but Vera beat her to it. 'I'll get her,' she called from the bedroom doorway.

Karin grimaced, half-listening to one of Roland's tales about his teenage children.

Isa carefully wiped her mouth with a napkin, then declared, 'Wet nappies, I bet.'

'I changed them an hour ago.' Karin had another forkful of salmon.

'Better feed her in that case.'

I'd never had to deal with a mother telling me how to be a mother. My mother had died in my childhood. What was it that made someone a mother? Or a father, for that matter? Was love itself enough? Quick, I reminded myself, look at the flowers. Smell the roses.

The howls increased as Vera reappeared, clasping Baby in her lilac crochet blanket. She was nuzzling the tiny, screwed-up face. I could see how desperate she was to hold on to the child and kiss away her tears, and yet she bent down and obediently delivered the bundle into Karin's outstretched arms.

I closed my eyes, bit into the fruit tartlet. The sweetness of cream, strawberry and short crust was filling my mouth when I heard Roland say casually, against a background of screams: 'Yeah, we've got a big garden. Danielle is fond of flowers – in moderation, though. Not like this.'

My eyes flew open. He was gesturing at my living room with his nearly empty wineglass: 'Must have cost a small fortune.' He gave me a sly nod. 'Yeah, a small fortune all right.' He was smirking now. 'You must sell lots of pottery.'

I looked away. The half-eaten tartlet slid through my fingers, down my skirt.

What the hell was he trying to do? Had the Chablis gone to his head?

Baby was still screaming. She was pummelling Karin's bare breast and bucking her small body like a creature about to be sacrificed.

Isa kept tugging at the crochet blanket, insisting, 'Nappies. I bet it's nappies.'

Karin yelled at her to shut up.

'Here, let me clean that for you.' Vera was squatting at my side with a dishcloth, her tailored dress all creased up. She dabbed at the smeary trail on my skirt, then lifted the tartlet's remains off the rug. I wondered if she'd caught on to what Roland was implying. 'It won't leave a trace, don't worry,' she said.

'Thanks, Vera. I'm not usually such a baby.' I tried to laugh. It was a feeble joke, but she smiled back as she straightened up. Remembering the orange pollen stains along the hem of her dress, I felt like hugging her – hugging her and shouting it all out, to be done with it.

When I glanced up, my eyes met Roland's.

'So?' he asked. He sounded drunk, and aggressive. I noticed his glass was full again. 'How *do* you manage to keep yourself in flowers like a funeral parlour?'

The sweet scent of the roses solidified into a pungent closeness that threatened to stifle me. Everything around me – the room, the air, the people, their quarrels, suspicions and accusations – seemed to coalesce into a cloying, grasping mass that I couldn't escape any more.

'I wasn't Michael's lover, if that's what you're thinking!'

The sudden silence was punctuated by Baby's suckling noises. They were all watching me.

I couldn't move. Roland was like a big cat crouched to spring. I saw his bloodshot eyes, saw the sofa quivering under Isa's weight, saw the golden hairs on Karin's arms, Baby's tiny finger-nails, the water dripping from the wet dishcloth in Vera's hand – I saw it all, and I couldn't move.

Roland grabbed the vase of roses and raised it high in the air: 'What about the flowers, then?'

I began to cry. I couldn't help it.

No-one said a word. They were waiting for me to break down properly and confess.

So I confessed.

But it wasn't what they had expected to hear. Not at all. Their faces were like mirrors. Showing their disbelief, their near-disappointment at first. Then their shock and outrage. Their jealousy. I was one of them, after all. Michael's eldest daughter. Born to the wife of his best friend Walter, who had loved me as his own.

I felt happy inside, despite my tears.

At some point, I took the vase away from Roland to cradle it in my arms. The roses smelled fragrant again, almost heady, and I tried to smile as I held on to them. The Japanese cherry tree was no longer visible beyond the window. Instead there was only us, reflected in the glass against the darkness outside. All of us together.

Everybody Goes Crazy
Once in a While

Country folk, I thought, would be kinder. But now they've barricaded my doors and windows from the outside, shutting me in like a wild beast. The police will be here soon.

Everybody goes crazy once in a while, don't they?

I can hear Jeanie yapping from Weekend John's doorstep up the lane, where she's guarding my things. There are muffled voices now, and shouts. The barking has stopped. Surely those men wouldn't harm my dog?

Forty, I told myself after my wife had divorced me and taken the kids, forty would be the cut-off point: either by then or never. So when I had the accident at thirty-nine, falling off a telescopic ladder and permanently injuring my back, I knew it was time.

I sold my bungalow in Sheffield, put my belongings into storage, traded in my car for a camper van, and set off in search of new beginnings.

The Scottish Borders seemed perfect: the air smelled sweeter, the people smiled when they greeted me, the houses were affordable, and Jeanie delighted in exploring the wonders of rabbit holes, true to her mixed Jack Russell and dachshund ancestry.

Jeanie is yapping again, frenziedly. Poor dog. What will happen to her if the police take me away? Maybe they really will lock me up and throw away the key as old McBain said. But I'm not a menace to the public – he's wrong about that.

The first time I came here, sixteen months ago, was one of the happiest days of my life.

'Excuse me!' I called out across a dry-stone wall into the rampant summer wilderness of a cottage garden from where I could hear laughter and the clink of glasses.

Jeanie was scuffling up on her hind legs to peer through a gap when two spaniels came pelting through the high grass on the other side and, spittle flying, lunged and barked at us.

'Stop it, boys!' A tall, floppy man had appeared from the back of the house, dressed in sun-bleached shorts and a sleeveless black T-shirt, and holding a half-full glass of red. At his approach, the spaniels sat back on their haunches, tongues lolling. 'Sorry about that,' he said with a smile. 'Their bark's worse than their bite.' The evening sun gave his face a handsome bronziness and made his white hair stand out halo-bright. Not that he was old – late forties at most.

I apologised for intruding, then explained I was interested in buying Briar Cottage in the side lane. Could he tell me when the McBains, who had a key, would be home?

The man swirled the wine round his glass. 'I've no idea. But hang on, I'll ask.' He returned to say his wife had seen them drive off a couple of hours earlier. 'That could mean anything, of course,' he commented. 'They're retired.'

I thanked him and stepped away from the wall. 'I'll take Jeanie for a walk and try again later. Or tomorrow if need be. My camper van won't mind.' I laughed, rather girlishly, and had to put a quick hand over my mouth.

The man wished me luck, adding that Briar Cottage could be 'a nice wee place with a bit of work'. Flanked by the spaniels, he started back towards the chatter of voices, then suddenly swung round again. 'Hey, why don't you join us? We're having a barbecue.' He grinned as he held out his hand. 'They call me Weekend John.'

I signed the contract for Briar Cottage at the beginning of October, ten days before my fortieth birthday.

What would Jeanie say, I wonder, if her barks could be translated into words? That she lost her sunny back garden in the city, her pals in the park? In exchange for what? A cottage which reeks of damp, breeds armies of woodlice, spiders and beetles that invade her bed, creep into her fur and drown in her water bowl? A cottage which required so many licks of paint it gave her lip a permanent curl of disgust and her coat a Disney dapple of cherry-blossom pink and silver-moon blue? A cottage whose fuchsia-red rugs, fuchsia-red cushions, fuchsia-red blinds give her nightmares? But dogs don't see colours, do they? Or would she talk about me? How, after settling down at last, I changed hair-styles, clothes, ornaments and took up the guitar again, singing softly, much more softly than before, moaning almost?

And Briar Cottage itself, what does it whisper to the wind at night, to the owl as its shadow touches the roof? Sometimes, lying in bed, I can hear a groaning in the old ceiling beams, a strained sighing in the walls as if the laths were short of breath, and sometimes there's the *ping* of a roof tile as it breaks in half.

Two days after my birthday I went to see my new GP, complaining of a (phantom) pain in my heart – not too far off the truth, after all. The doctor was fat and pleasant. So, during another appointment (for a nonexistent cough) I screwed up my courage and told him about the vows I'd made to myself in childhood whenever I glimpsed a falling star or caught the bigger part of a wishbone.

Not long afterwards I was sent to a female psychiatrist for weekly sessions.

'Why is it,' I asked her just before Christmas, 'that sadness produces such a clear liquid? Shouldn't sadness be murky, dark and troubled?'

She glanced at me without saying a word.

'You know,' I continued, 'I've started to collect my tears. I keep them in a small glass phial in my bathroom cabinet, next to the three flasks of perfume I've treated myself to: *Patchouli, Loulou* and *Opium.*'

This time, I'd grabbed her attention all right. She stared at me.

With my most sincere smile I said, 'Please give me a chance. A three-month trial of those pills would be enough for me to find out whether this is truly what I want.'

Her lips were pursed as she slid her gaze down my face – from undulating hairline, modest nose and mouth to generous expanse of chin – keeping well away from my eyes. Finally she shrugged and said she'd arrange for a referral to the local hospital, where they had a specialist to assess cases like mine.

When I thanked her, she shook her head quietly. 'Let's just wait and see, shall we?' she said. 'Meanwhile, take these.' And she handed me a pack of antidepressants.

The New Year cards I sent out were designed, printed and laminated in my very own office-cum-living-room – with a photo of Jeanie in a reindeer hat, holding a beribboned bone in her mouth, and a verse I'd written a few months earlier and tried unsuccessfully to turn into a pop lyric. Thanking everyone in the hamlet for their friendly reception of me, a virtual stranger, I said how grateful I was for being allowed at last to explore my own destiny. I signed with my new name: 'Michelle'.

A few days after Hogmanay, Weekend John and his wife arrived in their beat-up diesel VW, having escaped the city to spend their time battling with the temperamental old stove in their freezing cottage. I soon heard John's axe ring out in the cold, still air, punctuating the chatter of blackbirds, sparrows and chaffinches as they fought over the seeds on my kitchen sill. A quarter of an hour later I was ready for my walk with Jeanie.

'Happy New Year, John!' I leant my elbows on the dry-stone wall, and Laurel and Hardy, the two spaniels, bounded up for a biscuit each.

'Oh, hello … Michelle.' John straightened up and came over, leaving his axe stuck in a half-split log. 'And a happy New Year to you, too. Thanks for your card, by the way. Very professional-looking.' He patted the dogs, but he was grinning, thank God, his face flushed and shiny with sweat.

'Well –' I tucked back a strand of blonde hair from the wig I'd bought and my new gold bracelet tinkled '– if you're ever in need of desktop publishing services, you'll know where to come.' I squinted down at the flecks of ice on the stones in the wall which, even as I watched, seemed to form themselves into recognisable shapes, one of them an oddly familiar face in profile, with a large, square chin and a snub nose.

'Blonde suits you, I must say.' John's voice sounded admiring. He'd bent down to pick up a tennis ball, and Laurel and Hardy shot off.

'Thank you.' I smiled, just a little coquettishly. Then, with another tinkle of the bracelet, I pulled the present from my pocket. 'Something I would like you to have, John.' And I held out my black balaclava.

Jeanie leapt up to snatch it away. 'Jeanie, no!' I screamed at her, nearly.

John turned the hat over and over in his hands. Finally he said, 'That's very kind of you, Michelle. It'll certainly keep me warm – both outside and inside the cottage.'

'I'm so glad,' I blurted out. 'You see, I won't need it now.' I could feel myself blush. But there was nothing wrong with blushing like a girl, of course. Not any more.

Overnight, it seemed, the rowan tree in my back garden had flung on its bridal gear, the cream-white splashes vying with the sappy new green, bursting to let nature transform them from frothy nothings into heavy clusters of berry red.

To me it felt like a signal. I opened the wardrobe, bulging with my recent purchases from various ladieswear departments in the neighbouring town, and began to try on dresses, skirts, low-cut tops, turtlenecks, blouses, cardigans, stockings, then practised teetering about in my new, high-heeled ankle boots, with Jeanie scampering after me from room to room. Three days later I felt confident enough to go outside. Farmer Quin and the McBains did their damnedest not to ogle my fake-fur coat and satiny tights when we passed each other in the lane.

You're lovely, I keep telling myself, don't worry. Everybody goes crazy once in a while. Picture your soft, blonde curls reaching all the way down to your shoulders; picture your gold hoop earrings, your honey-coloured complexion courtesy of Revlon, your glossy-pink cupid-bow lips, your blue eyes shimmer-shadowed a deeper blue, your eyebrows plucked into sculpted arches; look at your nice, neat hands, at the bright red of your fingernails, hardly chipped; look at your slim hips and the straight, sturdy legs perfect for those high heels. A pleasing sight, don't you think? Especially when you smile like you're doing now, and the two dimples show in your cheeks. Cute, even at forty-one.

Yes, you have come far, achieving all this in only one year. Discovering the freedom of being yourself, exploring it so wholeheartedly, so totally, it's like living in a brand-new element.

Even your flesh feels different, softer somehow, more pliable, wanting so much to be touched. Your blood, too, seems different, thicker, more viscous, a deeper crimson – as you noticed the other day when you cut yourself by accident. Your taste buds have evolved and now discriminate between too much and too little salt, and you suddenly smell things you didn't before: stones hot from the sun, fresh rain on leaves, the brisk coldness of snow.

Maybe, of course, it's simply a matter of allowing yourself at long last the time and pleasure to care. And care you do. God, you wouldn't mind caring for others like you. Helping them to fulfil themselves.

After the DIY jobs necessary to spruce up Briar Cottage, I started on the suntrap back garden. Pruned the apple and plum trees, trained a young pear tree against the kitchen wall, dug over and planted the vegetable patch. Building a pond – an old dream of mine – was next, complete with a solar-powered fountain, ornamental stones, shells and marbles I'd collected over the years, exotic marsh plants and water lilies I hoped would serve as sun lounges for the local frog population. I wasn't disappointed. The pond attracted over a dozen frogs in the first month alone and I often watched them lazing about, flicking out their long, thin tongues with lightning speed whenever an insect or spider ventured too close. That was before the herons arrived.

I advertised my designer skills on several websites and in the shop windows of the nearby town. But producing the occasional church leaflets, take-away menus, community bulletins and business cards didn't keep me occupied. Nor did writing song lyrics for myself. Looking after Weekend John's straggly garden seemed the ideal project. His wife was so grateful that she called round one day and sat in my fuchsia-cushioned armchair, making small talk for a full hour while managing not to glance at my legs, which I'd forgotten to shave that morning.

The rowan berries have long since been pecked at by birds, blighted by rain, scattered by the winds, trampled and mashed underfoot by creatures of the night.

Autumn in these parts is dank and miserable if the mists won't lift. So I was glad to hear the rattle of the letterbox this morning, less than two hours ago. Picking up an airmail envelope from my daughter, who is to be married soon, I was even gladder. Then I read the message, which had travelled all the way across the chill Atlantic:

> Hey there, Dad/Michelle,
>
> Listen, I don't want to hurt your feelings but all things considered, I'd rather you didn't turn up at the wedding. Just imagine how awkward it would be for everyone… I am so sorry.
>
> Take care,
> Lots of love, Kirsty
>
> PS. Thanks for the money. It'll buy us a top-of-the-range Dyson.

I was halfway through a bottle of cognac when I saw a heron flap past the kitchen window and swoop down to the pond. Its long beak began to stab into the water, *my* water with *my* frogs, lovely, vulnerable frogs, *stab-stab-stab*, like a drilling machine.

I ran shouting into the back garden, pursued by Jeanie. At the same moment the heron lifted itself into the air, just missing Jeanie's teeth and banking sharply over my head in triumph and derision, with a soft, mottled body in its beak – the last of my frogs. My pond was dead now, black and dead. If I'd had a gun, I would have shot that bastard of a bird.

Instead I chased it. Out through the gate and into the drizzly morning emptiness of the village lane. I was still in my satin nightgown, and my feathery white slippers made hollow sucking noises on the wet cobbles. I kicked them off. Jeanie tried to retrieve them, but her mouth was too small for both and she ended up scurrying to and fro, yapping like a banshee.

The heron suddenly veered to the left and vanished behind some trees. I went on racing up the lane, unthinking and unstoppable now like a wind-up toy that's been kept in a box for too long.

The nightgown with its flounces billowed out behind me, a gleaming seashell pink in the watery dreichness. I whipped it off. Flung it down on Weekend John's doorstep together with my wig, the blonde hair stirring slightly in the damp breeze.

Fifty yards ahead, the school bus was idling at the corner.

I jogged up to it. The door had just slid shut behind the last straggle of children. The driver stared at me through the slowly swishing windscreen wipers, open-mouthed. The children craned their necks. Some of them sniggered. Others cheered. Still others shrank away, hiding their faces.

I know now I should have simply carried on and down the track between Farmer Quin's fields, pretending to be out and about, communing with nature.

Why didn't I? Why did I have to break my stride and hammer on the bus windows with my fists? Why did I have to shout, over and over again, 'Look at me! Just look at me, for pity's sake!'?

By the time the driver had recovered his wits and was revving the engine, sounding his horn to alert the villagers, my knuckles were bleeding and my voice had grown hoarse.

The bus pulled away so abruptly I landed on my hands and knees, just as old McBain came panting up the lane, swinging his gnarled walking stick.

To give him his due, he didn't hit me, merely poked me in the ribs as I got to my feet.

'Are you crazy?' he exclaimed. 'What do you think you're doing? In front of the kids, too! Be lucky if they don't put you on that sex offenders' list. And take off those stupid plastic tits. Just look at you! Ridiculous. Go home now and get dressed. Then stay put.'

His stick started to push and prod me like a farm animal back along the lane.

Jeanie was lying on top of my wig and nightgown, the slippers next to her. She grinned proudly and wagged her tail. 'Come here, Jeanie,' I called, but my voice was weak, sapless, and the dog didn't obey.

I am feeling better now. Everybody goes crazy once in a while, don't they? Underneath the kimono, my skin is slick with perfume, like a wrestler's body covered in oil: *Patchouli* for the legs, *Loulou* for buttocks and belly, *Opium* for arms, chest and throat. The bottle of cognac is empty and I've had to start on the vodka. The glass phial with my tears sits in the centre of the table, untouched.

Jeanie is howling, but she'll have to fend for herself; I can't help her now. In the distance there are sirens and, like a fire sucking in a sudden rush of oxygen, the voices in the lane outside build up to a roar.

I unstopper the phial, toast myself, then quickly tilt back my head to gulp down the contents. Now nothing will remain of me and my grief. My striving for a better self. A new life.

My neighbours have begun to tear off the boards they nailed across my door. I stand up, straighten my kimono and go into the hall, ready to greet them.

Meeting the Exiled Emperor

Moira was afraid. Not even the fact she was with Luna could take away her fear.

She could hear the dog padding along in the thickening darkness of the November evening, somewhere on the other side of the gorse bushes. To her right, the Royal Edinburgh Observatory crouched on the hilltop like a crested dragon, ready to hunt down the clouds scudding across the sodium haze of the city. The wind had grown stronger. Its gusts threw her off-balance and whipped the bushes into ragged shapes against the night sky, into dummies in flapping skirts and headscarves, gangs of swaying hoodies, hunchbacks ...

Get a grip, Moira told herself and put up the collar of her padded jacket. *Shielding myself.* She almost laughed at the thought – almost, but not quite – as another gust slammed into her. It was a courage thing with her, this walking in the dark. She was free now, floatingly, flyingly free. Nothing left to lose. *Nothing except myself.*

One of the gorse bushes, the hunchback ... It wasn't just being lashed into shape; it was moving – in her direction.

Moira stood frozen. Where the hell was Luna?

She tried to shout, but only a small sound came out, a whimper really, blown away by the wind like dust. She half-turned to keep an eye on the black figure of the hunchback, then forced her feet into action, one step at a time, towards the Observatory's lighted windows and the car park: left ... right ... left ...

The nearby gorse bushes cracked apart in a flash of white as Luna appeared, panting and wagging, a ball in her mouth. Moira acted instinctively. Prised it from her teeth and hurled it sideways, over at the hunchback. *Let's see how he'll deal with a hefty Labrador charging up to him.*

There was a scream, muffled by barks and the whining of the wind. When Moira risked a look over her shoulder, the hunch-

132

back was waving both arms in the air – a pretty stupid thing to do because Luna only jumped up higher, all the more ferocious in her playfulness. Next moment, the hunchback had disappeared and Luna was poking at something on the ground.

Moira sidled off. No need to get involved.

'Help me, please! Don't leave me. My ankle –' The cry was hardly audible, but something about it made Moira stop in her tracks. She shivered. Hadn't she heard that voice before? It seemed familiar, like a long-lost memory. Which was nonsense of course, because she did without memories these days; she'd got rid of all that. She was a woman of the new millennium, liberated, forward-thinking: a no-frills, no-fuss woman travelling light – just two suitcases, a holdall and a vanity case, her whole baggage fitting neatly into the boot of her car.

Moira lowered her head and carried on. Her fear was gone, for the present at least, and she even managed to whistle for Luna, loud and clear enough to cut through the wind and darkness.

It had taken her forty-one years to reach this point: someone else's dog trotting by her side, someone else's roof over her head and no rent to pay, no bills, no phone-TV-broadband package, no tax. She'd stuck out nineteen years of marriage – until the twins left home – to finally say: 'Screw you, Keith, I've had enough. Enough of your hard-man act. Your shouting and bullying; your fake smiles in public as you whisper "Fucking bitch". You *fucking coward* – you make me want to puke!' After that, she'd spent another year living alone to find out who she really was. And what she wanted from life.

Luna had run off again, back to where the hunchback with the voice from the past seemed to be squatting among the gorse like yet another stunted growth. All at once Moira's fear returned, blindsiding her. She felt its claws ripping right through her upturned collar, into the soft skin of her neck, tearing at the flesh. *What if the hunchback tries to hurt Luna?* The dog was her responsibility, for the next couple of weeks at any rate.

The wind funnelled up her boot-cut trousers, slapped her in

the face, stung her eyes and sucked the breath out of her mouth, but she didn't stop until she was within a few metres of him. Not a hunchback, of course, just a man with a bulky rucksack. Luna was lying beside him. The man's arms were locked around her neck and he was stroking her with one hand; in the other, he was holding some sort of needle.

Moira reeled back. She wanted to scream.

'Now, please, will you help me?' the half-familiar voice demanded. The laugh that followed was mirthless, more like a croak.

Was he a junkie? Moira stared at the face turned toward her. And as she stared, the flitting traces of broken moonlight revealed the shadowy features of someone she used to know – used to know quite well, in fact.

The memory of Witches' Pond hit her with a blizzard of rainbow colours and pounding psychedelic music. She staggered. For just a moment, it felt like she was again stumbling along the snow-covered banks of the pond with the others on that far-off Hogmanay, drunk and scared as hell. It had been a dark night, so very much darker than usual. And the darkness had become one with her fear.

As Moira dug her heels into the short, slippery grass, she saw the man's mouth stretch into a slow smile. Christ, had he recognised her?

'Nice, friendly dog you've got here.' Again the mirthless laugh. 'Very trusting.' The needle glinted as it descended on Luna's head, then travelled down between her eyes, towards her nose.

'Don't you dare … lay a finger on …' The words came out in a whisper, as weightless as ashes.

'What's your problem? You help me – I let your dog go. Simple.' A haughty voice and no laughter now, only a spiteful silence. That's when the memories began to boil up inside her, and the disgust. He hadn't changed one bit. Just like he used to be as a boy: an arrogant little prick with horn-rimmed glasses, dressed in a black waistcoat and obsessed with Napoleon Bonaparte. That was his nickname in their schooldays – Bonaparte – and he'd felt flattered, the dumb kid. Behind his back, they'd called him Boner.

'The dog first or I'll ring the police.' She could play games, too.

Bonaparte's eyes gleamed at her through the windy shreds of darkness before he shifted at last to release Luna and put the needle in his pocket.

'If you're really hurt, I'll phone for an ambulance, and then I'm away. I'm late already,' she added. No-one was expecting her, of course, but Bonaparte wouldn't know that.

The house was empty. A Victorian mansion in the Grange. All hers for the fortnight, with its high-ceilinged rooms, the wedding-cake scrollwork and chandeliers, the paintings with their mounted lights angled just so, the flat-screen TVs in their gold-plated frames, the marble fireplaces, the leather sofas and soft Persian rugs, the master bedroom with the timer-controlled SAD-lamp and coffee machine to wake up to in the morning.

'Don't leave me here.' Bonaparte stretched out an arm. 'Help me walk back to the Observatory, please. A taxi to A&E is all I need.'

Again his eyes gleamed in that unsettling way. A gust of wind snatched at his hair, making it float in wild tangles – like weeds streaming and swirling around a face underwater, moonlit black water below a jagged hole in the ice, not deep, but cold enough to kill.

Moira suddenly felt faint; no fight in her any more. She remembered now that he'd grown up fatherless and had sometimes boasted he was a direct descendant of Napoleon. She brought out her mobile and rang for a cab, then picked up the man's rucksack, heaved it onto her shoulders and pulled him upright.

'Let's move,' she said. 'It's freezing.'

Together they leaned into the wind. His arm felt like a vice around her neck.

The day she'd walked out on Keith, she'd stood in front of her bedroom mirror and stared at herself. The mirror had always been cruel, especially on mornings like that, with the ash trees stripped bare and the window unscreened. Harsh light exposed her body in all its exquisite sadness: the bony shanks, thickening waist, sluggish upper arms and too-small breasts with the nipples gone from luscious berry-red to a hard, leathery brown. It had struck her for the very first time that, although she couldn't turn back the clock, she could at least enjoy what was left of her life.

And here she was now, lumbered with Bonaparte, of all people. She didn't want to say another word to him. It was bad enough having to touch him and feel his body against hers, hear his gasping breath. He was limping badly and stumbled every so often like an old man.

'Reminds me of when I was an invalid.' Bonaparte was panting hard now and slowing down.

Moira dragged him on a little faster, but he wouldn't stop talking. 'I had trouble with my lungs in my teens.' It was just like when he used to bore them with his Napoleon talk and the only way to shut him up was to hit him. 'An accident on the ice, it was called – they bullied me and nearly drowned me. I never seemed able to get enough air after that. Horrible.'

Luna burst from a thicket like a rifle shot and, after a cursory snuffle, was off again.

Moira struggled on. With every step, Bonaparte's arm contracted around her neck. With every step, his wiry, untrimmed hair scraped against her cheek.

'I was sent to a boarding school in the Swiss Alps for a cure. Thanks to a gift from an anonymous benefactor – a fairy god-father straight out of Brothers Grimm.' He laughed his croaky laugh again.

Moira decided to ignore him until they got to the car park. Instead, she found herself blurting out: 'I'm homeless.'

She felt him flinch and, glancing up, she added. 'Of course, that's not how other people see it. My friend Teri, for example, says I'm a chancer playing with fire and that I'll *become* home-less.' But I prefer the bald truth. Don't you?'

No reply.

Teri had been furious with her when she told her she'd handed in her notice and cancelled the lease for her flat. As a social worker, all Teri could see were the dangers of going it alone, not the benefits, the joys of self-determination. Moira smiled, remembering her parting shot that night: 'Now that we have a new Parliament with women in positions of power, surely I can work towards my own kind of independence, don't you think?'

Only a few more metres and they would reach the Observatory's car park. 'I'm a professional dog-sitter,' she announced. 'No worries about owning things, and if I'm between dogs and houses, I've always got my sons' digs.'

Her small Renault seemed to beckon to her, its white surface reflecting the fractured moonlight like a smooth, glistening sheet of ice.

'Yes,' she heard him say. 'I know what it's like, not quite belonging.'

What the fuck does he mean? Sure I belong! Moira whistled for Luna, extra-shrill.

'This is me back in Scotland after years abroad – the Far East mostly,' he continued. 'That's where I learnt about healing, particularly acupuncture, and how you can tap into *chi*, the life force. Such a powerful thing that, the will to live. I've seen people come out of a coma after being treated. A bit like Lazarus, I suppose.' He sounded smug – too damn smug.

She could feel the old rage against him bubbling up inside her. 'Right, let's get you over to the Observatory. You can shelter by the gate. Taxi should be here any minute now.'

With Luna safely snapped on the lead and Bonaparte deposited by the front entrance, rucksack at his feet, Moira felt suddenly boisterous – footloose and fancy-free. Propped against the door like a collapsed umbrella, he looked like a sad apology for a broken-down emperor.

'Just as well you don't remember me!' she shouted back at him as she ran off into the wild embrace of the wind, getting whirled about and lifted almost off her feet, laughing and giggling like a schoolgirl while Luna jumped and leapt at her side.

But she didn't drive off; she didn't even go near the car park. She hid in the spiky shadows of some gorse bushes, huddled up to Luna's warm, solid body, and waited.

It wasn't long before the taxi arrived, pulling up close to the gate. She watched the driver help Bonaparte inside. Doors slammed and they began to move off, out of her life. *Thank God for that!*

She had just started walking towards the car park when Bonaparte leaned out of the window and yelled what sounded like: 'Till next time, Moira!' Then the taxi disappeared round the corner.

She stopped so abruptly the tautened lead jerked Luna to a halt. The wind, too, seemed to cease for a moment as she stood motionless, listening into the darkness and the silence, hearing nothing but the hammering of her own heart, her eyes searching out the Observatory's few lit windows, filling them with images from a child's Advent calendar, with teddy bears, dolls and angels, anything, to keep the brightness from being blotted out.

She knew that on her return to the house in the Grange she would go from room to room, from the cellar right up to the attic, and would switch on every single light.

Walking Down the Line

The day had started normally enough. Track inspector Mario Caflisch had got up at five-thirty to catch the 06.12 from Chur. The formation had been short: just a freight car, an ancient red carriage and the locomotive manned by Fredi, a taciturn Bernese who preferred his own company. Mario had been the only passenger and there was no ticket collector. No-one had boarded at Bergün. Everything as it should be. Casually, he'd glanced into the black mirror of the windowpane. He liked to think of himself as not bad-looking – late thirties and sturdily built, with an indestructible, tanned face that resembled the mountains he so loved, his eyes a clear glacier blue, his nose a little craggy, his skin as smoothly fissured as slate from his daily battles with the elements. But this morning he had hardly recognised himself in the rattling glass; all he'd seen reflected there was a barely suppressed rage.

Unbidden, his grandmother's tale about the changeling had come back to him:

'Once upon a time, on the night of the witches' Sabbath, a young mother fell into a deep slumber while watching over her baby boy asleep in his cradle ...'

The words had insinuated themselves in stealthy, evil whispers. Eventually he'd shut them out by concentrating on the *ra-ta-ta, ra-ta-ta, ra-ta-ta* of the wheels as the train jolted him along, in and out of the tunnels, underneath the avalanche galleries and over the viaducts, all the way up to the Alpine settlement of Preda. Meanwhile, the old window next to him had kept shuddering in its frame like something alive and half-frozen from the icy blasts that were pushing in through the rotted rubber seals.

After waving Fredi off, he'd watched the red tail lights disappear into the Albula Tunnel. Then he had filled his lungs with the snow-crisp mountain air and gazed up at the sky, seeking out Venus, his daily ritual before radioing Silvio at HQ to report for duty and starting his descent – 12.6 km divided into 60-cm steps, from sleeper to sleeper, 21,000 steps in all.

Everything had seemed routine later on, too. No major hold-ups. Some icicles needed knocked down under the humpbacked road bridge where the double tracks merged near Naz; the ballast had been scattered again by foraging foxes between the cliffs of Maliera and the Zuondra Tunnel, and there was the odd rock or tree branch that had landed too close to the rails. The usual trains passed at the usual times. Even the weather was normal: cold and sunless now that the day had truly begun. As always Viaducts IV and III made him feel on top of the world, spanning mountains with his steps, before he got buried once more in the 677-metre Toua Tunnel, the longest in this section and partly running underneath the Zuondra. At Maliera automatic block post he had a *Biberli* pastry and a swig of tea from his rucksack. Afterwards he must have walked on autopilot, because next thing he knew he was inside the Rugnux Tunnel.

And that was when he had seen the light moving towards him round the curve. For a moment he'd thought he was hallucinating. But he couldn't hear anything, none of that telltale thundering rush of compressed air, engine noise, metal screeching on metal and echo bouncing off the walls. There was no train due at this time, nor any maintenance vehicle or snow plough – it hadn't snowed for the past fortnight and the last few pockets of ice along the track had melted in the early spring sun. Still, out of habit, he had retreated to the nearest service niche where he now stood waiting in the dark, having switched off his power torch.

Mario shook his head. Who the hell could be trekking along his stretch of the railway line, courting danger? Certainly not another track inspector – no track inspector in his right mind would be trudging *up*hill, least of all the hazardous Bergün-Preda section. Should he radio Silvio? Should he call out a warning? Neither, he decided. He'd deal with the intruder in his own fashion. This was *his* territory.

Leaning against the tunnel wall, breathing in the familiar

draughty dankness of stone and eternal sunlessness, he could almost taste the raw blood smell released by the chafed iron, which seemed to cling to the air inside the tunnel.

Blood, he thought. If only there had been blood! A small wound, at least; just something to make it feel more real, less ghost-like, less like his grandmother's terrible fairytale. But there had been no blood. No tears. There had been nothing at all.

When he'd got home that March day four years ago, the house had been filled with the rich smells of a barley soup, his favourite, simmering away in the kitchen, and he had heard his wife (and childhood sweetheart) singing above the hum of the vacuum cleaner. He had rushed upstairs with an eager, foolish smile.

For only a fool could have believed that Anni had finally managed to lift herself free of the weary sadness she'd sunk into after the cot death of their little boy. Only a fool could have mistaken the ominous tune for a song: two notes up, one note down, two notes up, one note down, higher and higher until her voice reached breaking point, broke and dropped like a bird shot in mid-flight, then started up again, two notes up, one note down...

Following the sounds along the corridor, he had lost his smile and begun to tiptoe. Slowly he'd sneaked past the bedroom, past the bathroom, on towards the spare room with the teddy-bear wallpaper.

Anni was by the window, vacuuming the same patch of sun-splashed blue carpet, over and over. Already it seemed to have a worn and threadbare look, utterly lustreless. Just like the eyes she turned on him when at last he found the courage to approach her and say, 'Anni, dear, come on, I'll make us a cup of coffee, shall I?'

He bent to kiss her, but she twisted away, gave him a hard, empty stare, then stated flatly: 'Go away, I have work to do.' Resuming her tune, she stepped round him and continued with her task of cleaning the sunlight off the carpet. In the end, he had drawn the curtains and held her, held her tight until the doctor arrived and took her away.

The memory of it made him feel angry yet again. Angry with the doctor and with himself for not realising what had been happening to Anni, angry with his grandmother for foretelling it all in her story and, in effect, fating it.

Mario wiped his eyes with the back of his hand. Dammit, he was a grown man and it hadn't been his fault, had it? He had tried, really tried, to help Anni. But she had refused to have another child, and every time he'd started to talk about things she'd changed the subject or simply walked off. He still visited her now and then, though she no longer recognised him. 'Your wife has imprisoned herself in her own mind,' the doctor had told him, 'and unless she decides to open the door, well, I'm afraid...'

Just like being stuck inside a tunnel, Mario thought, with a shiver that had nothing to do with the damp and cold around him. To be honest, he was beginning to feel trapped. And worried. The Rugnux Tunnel burrowed into the mountain in a single spiral turn of 661 metres, which meant that due to the curve and gradient the stranger couldn't have been more than a 150 steps away – so where was he now? What if the man had seen *his* torchlight and hidden same as him, each now waiting for the other? But there would be a train soon, the RE 1124, and Mario didn't want a death on his hands. He was about to set off when a light came wavering along the rails and footsteps crunched awkwardly into the ballast, having missed the sleepers. Mario flipped on his torch and burst from the service niche with a shout.

The intruder let out a high-pitched cry, stumbled and dropped his flashlight, which briefly illuminated the tunnel wall, then came to rest against the rail, catching in its beam not a man but – Mario breathed out with a hiss – a woman!

'Don't hurt me, *signore*.' An *Italiana*. Hooded and shielding her face behind pink mittens. Mario pulled her hands away. She was young, with large, deep-set eyes and clenched teeth, the rest of her features distorted into a grotesquery of lines, planes and shadows by the torchlight.

'No-one is going to hurt you, but you'll have to come with

me. There will be a train soon.' His Italian sounded rusty even to him. He hadn't spoken it much since Gino, his best friend and workmate, had moved back to Poschiavo a few years earlier.

'But I've lost my earring!' Fumbling with the hood of her sheepskin coat, the *Italiana* indicated first a pierced and unadorned earlobe, then a single milky globe dangling from the other. '*Per favore*, I must find my earring. I still had it when I entered the tunnel. It's from my great-grandmother – *un portafortuna*, you understand?'

'*Sì, sì*, a lucky charm.' Mario recalled only too well the mossy-soft baby hair in the silver locket that his wife wore on a chain around her neck – a millstone in disguise. He grabbed the woman roughly by one arm and about-turned her. 'This way now,' he ordered, pointing down the track. Then he added more gently, 'I'll have a look for your earring tomorrow, okay?'

There was nothing she could do but nod. And nod she did; he was too strong for her and, frankly, she wasn't keen on being blasted away by the next express. She followed the man, trying to adjust her steps to the sleepers, without much success. He seemed trustworthy – the far side of thirty and an ordinary rail worker, from woolly dwarf's hat to steel-capped boots, clad in neon-bright orange with luminescent strips around arms and legs to keep him safe. Safety, of course, was one of the buzzwords in this dull little country. She smiled, fingering the 'missing' moonstone earring in her coat pocket, and her lips curled faintly with contempt as she listened to him and his erratic accent.

'Railroad tracks are dangerous. They're not public footpaths. There are laws, and you can be fined,' the man lectured her. 'How did you get here anyway, and why?'

'What's your name?' she asked to buy some time.

'Mario. And yours?'

'Clàudia, Sofia, Gina – take your pick.'

When he didn't respond, she allowed herself another smile in the dark, then launched into her spiel: 'Just doing research, Mario.

I've always loved trains, and this line's one of the most spectacular achievements of civil engineering. I wanted to pay tribute to it. Wanted to touch the tunnel walls and walk across the viaducts, walk every step of the way in memory of my compatriots who built it, a century ago, and –' She broke off. Had the man noticed she'd been larding it on a bit? Was this why he now remained silent, letting his torch beam play over the rails, walls and cables like a goblin's lighthouse beacon?

If he was so thorough in checking things, he must surely have found the camcorder backup battery she'd lost somewhere further up the tunnel – yet he would never suspect the truth. Not in a million years. Nothing except avalanches had ever threatened this Alpine hinterland where people passed through, mostly. But that was about to change…

'And why are you *really* here?' Was he a mind reader?

To help 'Genoa 2001' get their revenge, she could have replied. The group had said they weren't going to kill anybody, and that had been good enough for her. They were anti-G8 activists, after all – not terrorists.

'So?' the man persisted.

She looked at the glow of his outline in front of her, at the silver security strips shimmering in the torchlight. A guardian angel, it occurred to her: he was the guardian angel of the railways. This was probably the very first time he'd met a living soul wandering these tunnels. Plenty of ghosts haunting them, and no mistake.

'I've already told you, Mario –' she did her best to sound persuasive '– I'm a researcher and a fan – a railway junkie.'

Her own great-grandfather had been blown up somewhere along this track. Her *nonna* used to tell her the story when she was little, and in her story the tunnels were big, black, gaping mouths that needed their human sacrifices every so often or the mountains would start trembling with anger and the tremors would dislodge rocks and boulders, sending them crashing on to the people below, maiming and killing at random.

'I don't believe you,' the man retorted bluntly.

She shrugged to herself and said nothing. Poor *Nonna*, born in Preda a few months before her father died in a dynamite accident. That was back in 1901 when Preda was home to hundreds of Italian labourers and their families, proclaiming itself a 'town of the future' complete with church, hotel, kindergarten, barracks, workshops, warehouses, hospital and mortuary…

All of a sudden the man spoke into the radio strapped to his chest, something in Swiss German. Was he ratting on her?

'*Avanti.*' Still swinging his torch rhythmically from side to side, he had quickened his step. The end of the tunnel was curving into view and pallid snow light infiltrated the stony darkness, wreaths of mist that reminded her of the tattered shrouds of dead men.

The air outside tasted so fresh and cold it felt almost solid in her mouth, like *gelati*. Breathing in long, greedy gulps of it, she tried to ignore the roar of the river in the gorge far below as they traversed yet another viaduct, and she lifted her eyes up to the snow-covered peaks that rose steeply on either side, towering above like the menacing heads of the giants in her *nonna*'s tale. From higher up the valley came a keening that seemed to shatter into echoes as it got ever closer, then was abruptly silenced before swelling into a howling screech from deep within the mountain. As soon as they reached terra firma again, she swerved off the track into the brittle snow.

The train burst from the tunnel portal with sparks flying off the cables and rails, thundering across the viaduct towards them like a fiery monster. Even from a distance she could feel its inhuman pull and power. It turned the nearby fir trees into twitching marionettes that showered her with snow pellets; it slapped her jeans against her legs and blew her hood down, wire-whipping her hair about her already sore face. Her whole body reeled from the onslaught.

Gazing after the last of the freight cars in the drab daylight, she wasn't aware at first of the man's stare. Then she smiled, waited a beat, and said, 'Seen enough?' He quickly glanced away and marched off. Under his tan, his cheeks had reddened. She knew she wasn't a pretty sight with her swollen nose and bruised left eye courtesy of that bastard Antonio and his attempts to stop her from coming here.

After a while the man called out: 'See the animal tracks? These are from a hare, those by the trees from a fox.' He had halted and was staring again. She stared right back, unsmiling this time, until he shoved off once more. She put on her sunglasses. What was it with this guy? Yes, dammit, she'd been knocked about, but she'd given Antonio as good as she'd got, kneeing him twice in the groin. That had been the end of their affair. Antonio was married anyway, and two months with the same lover was quite enough. Better to keep moving, get to know new people, new places, new things. That's why she had specialised in the history of Italian migrant workers, including their role in the building of the Rhaetian Railway. And why she had agreed to this secret 'mission' – a one-off, she'd told Paolo, the leader of 'Genoa 2001'. All they wanted was some video footage of the line, particularly the tunnels, from Preda down to Filisur and over to Davos. She was the perfect spy: an innocuous academic on a project trip, and a woman with a personal agenda.

No, Mario thought, he couldn't bear walking with the *Italiana* in tow much longer, not in this awful silence that kept reminding him of Anni's withdrawal. Maybe it was a woman thing, punishing by silence and sheer indifference. He would have liked to point out the birds along the track, birds that seemed to recognise him, waiting for his approach on the same branch of the same tree every day, then circling overhead with harsh cries that clawed at the bright icicle sky. Mario blinked up at the snowy mountains. As usual they kept their own frozen counsel, and although he loved them, loved the very essence of them, their stillness, their immutability and permanence, today he felt suddenly insulted by their eternal aloofness. He stopped himself just in time from shouting 'Fuck you!' and shaking his fist at them. At the *Italiana* too, with her arrogance, her stupid lies. Even at Anni in her cool, shaded room at the clinic… Yes, at Anni! Most of all at Anni, goddammit! Theirs wasn't a relationship any more, let alone a marriage!

For a moment there was a haze in front of his eyes, but his feet moved on regardless, like those of a wind-up toy, from sleeper to sleeper. When his vision cleared, Mario was shocked at the violence of his feelings; they seemed to belong to someone else, not him. Little by little, he forced them down again, as if pushing a cork back into a bottle. Anni, poor Anni. He would visit her later today, in the hope that four years of stalemate was enough punishment for them both and that she'd finally call him by name once more.

Mario trudged on steadily. The sleepers stretched out ahead like so many stepping stones guiding him safely home. He'd be able to get shot of the woman very soon now. Muot Station, where he normally had his morning break, wasn't far; from there he'd radio in a request stop for the next train down to Bergün and pack her off, end of story.

'*Signore*, you must find all sorts of things in these tunnels, *vero?*'

At least she was talking. He answered her while mechanically scanning the track, sleepers and catenaries ahead. '*Sì*, sometimes nice, sometimes not. It's sad when animals get killed or injured by the trains.' He paused, wondering if she was still listening, then continued. 'But I've also picked up coins, two- and five-franc pieces tossed out for luck, once a silver ring engraved with a heart, another time a crucifix. And today, in the Rugnux – that's the tunnel behind us – I came across a rechargeable battery. Some weirdo, no doubt!' He laughed – and was glad to hear the *Italiana* join in. Out of delicacy he had omitted mentioning the occasional discarded condom.

Mario looked at his watch, then radioed Silvio to check on the next train – five minutes late, he was informed, because of an electrical fault at Bergün. He hadn't told Silvio about the woman yet. He'd wait until the RE 1128 was due in three quarters of an hour. Right now there was just enough time to get across the side viaduct and through the short Fuegna Tunnel and Gallery.

'We'd better hurry.' He glanced round at her. Despite the overcast sky, she was wearing sunglasses. All of a sudden he blurted out, 'Who the hell did that to you? Who hurt you?' Afterwards he could have bitten off his tongue.

The *Italiana* remained silent until they had entered the dark mouth of the mountain. Then her voice rang out, proudly, 'I hurt him back, don't worry!'

Mario cleared his throat and walked on a little faster towards the diffuse daylight. She was a woman with baby-pink gloves, he reminded himself, and a lot smaller than him. But he felt relieved when they emerged into the open. From down Val Tisch Viaduct he could hear the metallic screeches and sighs of the delayed train ascending towards them. The small wooden structure of Muot Station, well maintained though no longer inhabited, was another hundred metres ahead. It resembled a cosy little gingerbread house with carved green shutters and decorated eaves. He was on home ground now.

'Time for a break,' he announced, unlocking the door. He ushered the *Italiana* inside. 'Just make yourself comfortable; the kitchen's at the back.'

A minute later the train cleared the automatic block post and Mario gave the driver the customary wave, then stood watching from the threshold as the carriages blurred past. The floor trembled under his feet and seemed to go on trembling even after the last of the freight cars had disappeared. When he entered the kitchen, he pretended not to notice the woman's mobile on the table nor the sunglasses still hiding her eyes. Not so brave now, was she? He grinned to himself and for a fleeting instant glimpsed again, reflected in the tinted lenses of her glasses, that unfamiliar face from the train window.

With the fan heater on, the room warmed up quickly and the *Italiana* took off her coat, revealing a tight-fitting woollen sweater. She declined his offer of sandwiches and rosehip tea, and produced her own thermos of coffee, a couple of chocolate-chip pastries and a hip flask of *grappa*. Mario had the smallest of swigs, to be polite – he was on duty, after all. The woman made him feel restless. There was a sultriness about her he hadn't been aware of before. He wolfed down the first of his ham and gherkin sandwiches, then got up and strolled over to the window next to her.

'The deer are hungry, too,' he said with a forced laugh. When the *Italiana* turned in her seat, he pointed to the area of muddied snow around the plastic barrel he'd placed a short way up the mountain. 'I feed them old bread from the baker's.'

'That's nice.' She had more *grappa*.

He sat down again. Frowning, he chewed on his second sandwich, then mumbled, 'For the record, I never walk down this line without thanking the labourers who built it.'

She seemed to wince, but he must have imagined it because moments later she smiled, pushed up her sunglasses and lifted the *grappa* in a silent toast. As if on cue, her mobile beeped. She grabbed it, read the message with flying eyes and, after a furtive glance at him, texted back a reply.

'Just a friend,' she remarked, biting into her pastry so hastily she had to cough.

Boyfriend more like, thought Mario and leaned over to tap her on the back, careful not to let his hand linger.

'You've come well-prepared, haven't you?' he prompted her once she had recovered.

She merely gulped down more coffee, licked the pastry flakes off her fingers and started shuffling one of her scuffed boots to and fro on the carpet.

He had a sip of tea. Then another. And another. So she wasn't going to speak, was she? Fine. Time to get rid of her.

He was about to step outside to radio in the request stop when the sun broke through the clouds. It burst into the room with the raw, violent light peculiar to spring and bleached a pale rectangle into the carpet by the *Italiana*'s chair. The woman kept shuffling her boot as if nothing had happened. Kept moving it right across the splash of sunlight, over and over, until the carpet there seemed to him quite worn and threadbare, utterly lustreless and terrifyingly familiar. Mario felt despair surge up inside him, a tide that threatened to obliterate all he had ever been or ever would be, leaving him trapped in the purgatory of an eternal present. He tried to see out of the window and calm himself with the sight of the mountains, but something obscured his view, a cloud shadow that…

…and suddenly the man was springing at her. She scrabbled in vain for the mobile as she leapt to her feet, then began to back away. He looked different, somehow. No longer trustworthy. No longer the ordinary, conscientious rail worker, but a creature with overbright eyes and hands that clenched and unclenched with a barely restrained fierceness.

'What's wrong?' she shouted, her elbows braced against the windowsill so she could kick him if he came any nearer. 'Mario, no! No!' His orange outfit seemed to flare like a fire taking hold – and for an instant she was blinded by the image of her great-grandfather the railway builder and labourer, his body erupting in fragments, in bloodied shreds of flesh and fabric and shards of bone which were pounded and ground by tons of rock as he was annihilated in a blast that left only dust and rubble behind. A trail of tears ran down her cheeks.

When at last she dared open her eyes, her sunglasses lay shattered on the dirty blue carpet between the man's steel-capped boots. His fingers were digging into her shoulders and she could feel him staring at her. He was shaking her, saying things in Swiss German, addressing her as Anni.

Just then, over on the table, her mobile sang out the first notes of *Cosi Fan Tutti* – not Paolo again! The man spun round so abruptly they both tumbled to the floor, her head wedged painfully beneath his arm. She started to scream and struggle

... and that was when he seemed to wake from his madness, or whatever it was, as if the fire of viciousness had finally burnt itself out. The mobile had fallen silent, *grazie a Dio*!

She didn't bother to respond to his feeble excuses which all involved his wife – why was it that men always blamed their weaknesses and cruelty on women? Poor Eves and Helenas and so-called witches! Stuffing the mobile and the flasks into her rucksack, she seized her coat and left him and his hangdog expression standing there.

She was about to plunge headlong into the snow-and-sun glare outside when she remembered Paolo's pepper spray in the front pocket of her rucksack. The door to the dusty little waiting room was ajar, a large key in the lock. She went in.

Soon enough the man came barging in after her, imploring her to hear him out. She smiled and nodded, beckoned him closer. Then, with a *'Scusi, amico!'* she pressed the spray's lever. He raised his hands too late and screamed, his eyes already streaming as she unclipped the radio from his chest. He tried to follow her out, wiping at his swollen eyes, but she shut the door in his face and turned the key. He started banging and launching himself at the panels, yelling at her. Wood splintered as the rusty old hinges loosened in their frame.

She grimaced to herself, then examined the radio and quietly removed the batteries. Just in case.

'Listen, Mario. We'll do a deal!'

The frantic attacks stopped. 'Open up first, goddammit!' He sounded near crying.

'Here's the deal: if you swear not to tell anyone about me and let me carry on walking down the line without hassle, you can have your radio back. I'll forget about going to the police with my black eye and saying you did it. How's that?'

'But you assaulted me just now!'

'Self-defence, *amico*.'

'Open the door, dammit!'

'Only if you swear on your wife's grave.'

'She isn't dead. Anni is not dead!' Now he was crying outright.
'Whatever. Swear on her name, then.'

Mario's eyes were streaming and he could hear himself bawling
like a child. The pain seemed to radiate through his entire body, a
burning, searing pain that left him quite limp and helpless. Even
his heart felt sore. For a moment he fancied he was back in the
room of his baby son, hunched over his cot, over the terrible
stillness of his face…

He was about to say 'Anni' when there was a rumble
outside that grew louder and louder as the train from St Moritz
approached and, shaking the wooden structure of the station to
its very foundations, thundered past – and with it his chance of
sending the *Italiana* down to Bergün. In the silence that followed,
his sobs began to sound unreal and it occurred to him that his
'deal' with the woman was yet another stalemate: her threat pitted
against his. Within its balance lay what little freedom remained.

Nothing left to lose, nothing left to lose… The words came
to him out of nowhere, whispered over and over until he thought
he recognised the voice. He shrank from it.

Mario.

He crossed himself.

Grow up, Mario. You've got it all wrong.

He covered his ears, but it made no difference.

*That tale about the changeling – it isn't about your dead son.
It's about you, Mario. You!*

Mario laughed. He laughed so hard he was in tears all over
again.

'Okay?' he heard the *Italiana* ask through the door.

'No!' He caught his breath. 'Yes! No! Yes!'

Suddenly the rage he had felt earlier returned, only much
fiercer now, like a physical presence lashing him on as he
scrambled about, half-blind, shouting and screaming. Screaming
and shouting, he wrenched the old fire extinguisher from the wall.

Then he batter-rammed the door.

152

'Yes!' Every blow he struck, every crack and gash brought him closer to what was waiting for him on the other side. 'Yes! Yes! Yes!' He wasn't going to do anybody's bidding any more. Wasn't going to be anybody's slave. Not – ever – again.

When the railway police checked Muot Station later that day, they found it unlocked and vandalised. Apart from his service radio, which had been smashed to pieces, there was no trace of Mario Caflisch, one of their most reliable track inspectors.

The Marilyn Monroe of the Meadows

Breathing has become a chore. Climbing the stairs is like drowning. Every landing is a little island that invites you to collapse against the wall. Every mat is your mat. Every door your door. You're not smiling much these days, just blowing your white cheeks in and out so they make small popping noises. You're still beautiful and your eyes are still bright, rimmed with black as if you were already in mourning for yourself. The old ladies in the park call you the Marilyn Monroe of the Meadows.

'Old doggie, old doggie, funny old doggie,' the little boy says to his mother, then takes a running jump on to his scooter, whooping and waving to her as his flying foot pushes away the ground.

The mother looks round at us, smiles. Stops for a moment to give you a pat before hurrying off after her little boy, who's miles up ahead, not heeding her shouts. Heeding only the wild blur of freedom as it rushes to meet him.

We trundle on. Every step several heartbeats. I stare down at the mottled pavement around my boots, at the stains of ancient chewing gum and fresh spit. Then up at the sun, cold and wintry behind the bare trees and high sandstone walls. Some of the stones have eroded into a semblance of wood. Gouged by squalls of rain, splintered by frost, they appear scabrous and brittle in the harsh afternoon light, like the bark on the trees. Meanwhile you set down each paw with slow carefulness, swaying a little as if you were drunk. But always moving forward, stubbornly, like there is no way back. No way back home.

'Bonnie!' someone cries. A woman has emerged from the café opposite, dressed in a red and white striped apron. It's Grace. She always greets you first. I get a half-smile if I'm lucky.

Veering abruptly towards her, you nearly stumble over the

kerb and into the path of an oncoming car. I give a tug at your lead, but you strain against it, your breathing laboured now, your eyes with that glazed, determined look I remember from years back when you were a puppy, all wilful, chubby and frolicky.

'Old, isn't he? A retriever, right?' The car has slid to a standstill without my noticing, a silver Jaguar, and the driver's leaning out of the window. His meaty face is glistening with complacent bonhomie.

I nod, then quickly glance away, gritting my teeth as I begin to guide you across the street, on a short lead now. I know he'll study you like a judge at a dog show. Critically. Pitilessly. His eyes lingering on your frail shrunken lower jaw, the withered muscles of your hind legs, the tail trailing on the dirty tarmac, the general unsteadiness of your every step.

By the time we reach the other side I feel you've been skinned and boned alive. You're panting so hard your teeth are bared in a ghastly travesty of a grin, and your eyes seem to be starting out of their sockets. There is a homemade cheese scone in Grace's hand. At least your greed is undiminished.

'Hello, Grace,' I say, in a voice that's pretend-upbeat and easy.

'What a beauty you are, Bonnie. And so loving. So loving,' she murmurs as she struggles to embrace you with both arms while you guzzle the scone and lick the crumbs off the pavement.

I gaze down at the top of her head, the brown hair streaked with grey. Gaze down at the generous expanse of her bosom and thighs under the striped apron. 'So loving,' she repeats, before straightening up with a sigh. 'Sorry,' she says hoarsely, 'I got carried away there.'

We smile at each other.

Next moment an engine revs behind me and a horn is sounded, brashly, twice. You don't react at all, you're still busy cleaning up the pavement, but Grace jerks her head in the driver's direction, her eyes small and flat once more.

I don't turn round until the car has pulled away. I hope Meat Face will die of apoplexy.

The Pakistani owner of the grocer's shop on the corner must have seen us approach in the old wing mirror he has fixed to the wall opposite the till to watch passers-by, because he is already in position, miming the usual jokey kiss. I grimace mockingly in reply. We always go through the same ritual, though I've never been inside the shop, let alone spoken with him.

Moments later you retch, lurching against me violently. I almost lose my balance. You retch again, a shuddering gasp that produces nothing. Your sides are heaving with the effort to breathe; your tail's between your legs; your jaw has gone quite slack. Beads of moisture have appeared at your nostrils and scatter on the paving stone in small wet patches, like tears.

When I look up at last, the man is still there behind the shop window. He is gesturing to us to go in. But you won't move, merely stand gazing up at me dolefully, trembling and pressing your weight against my legs – as if I could walk for you, breathe for you. For an instant we remain like this, and I imagine it's really *you* supporting me. Then I bend down to gather you up in my arms, staggering. You're all of four and a half stone, I'm barely seven.

With a jangle the door is flung open. 'Poor dog. Is ill, yes? Come in, please, come in.' The man's voice is husky, just as I expected.

He shrinks away from your panting mouth and points towards a hallway at the back of the shop. 'You go there, is okay.' His black eyes are strangely pleading. That's when I realise he is afraid of you.

The small storeroom smells of spices; its walls are stacked with boxes, bottles, cans and tins. As soon as I put you down, you sink to the floor.

I squat next to you. Touch you. The fur over your skull is stretched tight.

The man edges round us gingerly to switch on the electric fire in the corner.

'You're very good to us,' I mumble. 'Thank you so much.'

He shrugs, smiles. His skin is the colour of cinnamon. He is older than I thought, early forties at least, with the beginnings of a double chin and a fine mesh of wrinkles round his eyes. His face is broad and pitted slightly, perhaps from teenage acne, and there's a dab of zinc cream on the side of his nose.

He is hovering uneasily, darting glances at the heavy rise and fall of your chest and back to me again. As if, at a snap of my fingers, you might leap up, miraculously restored, and pounce on him.

'She's very friendly,' I say, stroking your muzzle.

'Ah.' He frowns.

'Her name is Bonnie.'

Your ears twitch, very faintly.

'Ah.'

After frowning some more, he suddenly grins down at me: 'Like *Bonnie and Clyde*?'

I force a smile.

He indicates a chair, then the kettle beside him. 'Tea for you?'

'No, no. I'm fine, thanks.' I brush some dust off my coat and sit down, giving him another smile. 'If it's all right, I'll just stay here until she has recovered. Could she have some water, maybe?'

'Of course, of course.'

But you twist your head away from the little red plastic cup, without blinking your white eyelashes. Surely you must be thirsty after that cheese scone?

The man's gaze keeps flickering over me. 'I'm Mobin,' he says.

'Heather,' I respond, automatically.

He clasps my hand in both of his and I am glad when the door jangles up front, announcing a customer.

Later we trundle on even more slowly – and against my better judgement. But you are determined. You're aiming for the Meadows, which in your mind are no doubt eternally patrolled by the kindly old ladies with their spaniels and terriers, their love of Marilyn Monroe, and their pocketfuls of biscuits. So I humour you.

Although it's only down a short street, the park now seems a thousand heartbeats away. The sun has disappeared behind the roofs of the tenements. There's a duskiness in the air and a cold dampness that cuts to the bone.

From the nearby primary school, parents and boisterous children are streaming towards us. Engulfing us. You ignore them all. You are no longer bothered about being talked to or admired, concentrating instead on every faltering step.

'Poor old thing. Not too well, is he?' A hand with pale-green fingernails slips along your fur as you amble past.

I've never stared at the ground so hard, never given such a convincing impression of being deaf, and dumb.

'Why's his face all white, Mummy?'

Car doors begin to slam.

'Race you!' A sudden rush of boys' feet in chunky trainers. 'Our dog's much faster. Millions faster!' Followed by raspberries, sniggers and yells.

'Gie him a pat, girls, he looks a canny auld beast.'

Crumpled sweetie wrappers, tissues, cigarette butts, further on some dog turds and a half-eaten kebab.

When I let you off the lead under the big trees on the park's perimeter, you remain motionless for a moment, your head raised in the direction of the tennis courts, your black nose quivering. But there is no sign of the old ladies with their dogs.

Just then comes a distant burst of high-pitched barks.

You take a few steps into the park, hesitate, and look up at me.

Straining my eyes, I can pick out two familiar shadowy forms – one taller, wider, the other small like a child – and those of their dogs, retreating towards Middle Meadow Walk. Too far for you. Too far for them to hear my shouts.

You are still looking at me, more mournful than ever. As if I could compress space and time and make those ladies be here with us now, their smiles bright in the gloom, their hands bustling with kindness.

We stand gazing at each other until the gold of your fur merges with the failing light and the dark layer of leaves underfoot. Your white face seems unreal, ghost-like. In the end you totter off, vaguely sniffing here and there but refusing to pee. Withdrawing yourself from the community of park dogs. You seem in a daze.

'Bonnie?' I tap you gently on the head. 'Let's go home.'

You eat my biscuit almost wearily as I put you back on the lead.

We've started to move off when a black shape gallops up from behind, a frisky collie. But his presence barely registers with you, and after a cursory inspection he trots off.

The streetlamps are grimy smears against the grey tenement walls, the grey roofs, the grey sky. We're waiting for the pedestrian lights to change. Our days of happy jay-walking are over. Your breathing rasps in and out and all I can do is scratch you behind the ear as I watch the red man on the other side being erased every few seconds by buses and vans. My heart feels ragged inside me.

'Hello there!' It's one of our neighbours, an elderly lady with a fondness for yellow scarves and the glint of brooches.

'Oh, hello.' I make my lips curve upwards, briefly.

'I hope you don't mind me asking, but what's wrong with Bonnie? She has really slowed down, hasn't she, within the last couple of weeks?'

'Lung cancer,' I say, in a tone that's meant to close the subject.

The green man has come on. It's easy for her to keep up with us. 'Oh, I'm sorry. I had a friend whose dog, a Lab I think it was, though I'm not sure, might have been a Heinz 57, you know, but mostly Lab,' she pauses as I coax you up onto the kerb, 'yes, now *that* dog had water on his lungs and the vet gave him some pills, diur-something, and the dog lived for years after that, years and years.'

How dark it is getting, an ashy darkness that seeps into my mouth, my nostrils. Stifling me. I tug at your lead, tell you to stop for a minute.

Our neighbour's already a few steps ahead and peers over her shoulder with a baffled expression.

I simply glare at her.

'Well, I'd better be going. Sorry about poor Bonnie.'

I want to scream at her to stuff her bloody sympathy, I don't need it, thanks very much. Nor does Bonnie. I am shaking with a cruel, impotent rage. The tears are hot on my face as I bend over you, lift your silky ears to my eyes and whisper your name, over and over, while you stand there impassively, reeling ever so slightly.

Along this side street and we'll be home. Without warning, you keel over, flat onto your side. Your eyes are glassy, staring at the garden wall a metre away.

'Bonnie!' I crouch down next to you.

'Bonnie!' I stroke you.

'Bonnie!' I lay my head against yours.

'Bonnie!' I fumble a biscuit from my coat pocket. 'Here, Bonnie!'

You don't react. But you're not dead. Your flanks are shivering as you shallow-breathe, each breath taking all your strength. I wish I'd brought my mobile. Because this time there's no shop window. No friendly Pakistani man. No-one holding open a door. It's just you and me and an invisible blackbird trilling away in the garden behind the wall, and the early winter darkness falling all around us.

I can feel my face getting screwed up. A car passes, accelerating sharply, probably at the sight of us.

'Everything's going to be all right,' I say. 'Everything.' I kiss you on the nose and your tongue attempts a feeble lick.

Then I hear footsteps and a tall, pleasant-looking woman with books under her arm turns the corner. She is fiddling with her mobile. I'm about to call out to her when she abruptly crosses the street, away from us.

But you're not dead, whatever she may think. You're not dead.

We'll have to wait for a Good Samaritan now. Huddling up to you, I can feel the flutter of your heart, and I lay my head there and cry. Things are drawing in: the year, the month, the day.

Your fur is wet from my tears when we finally get home, thanks to a scruffy young man who offered his help without being asked.

You don't know that from now on everything will happen for the last time. You retch, gasp and pant as your last visitors crowd round to show you their affection, caressing your ears between their fingers. Then you have your last few pills (painkillers, not miracle workers, hidden inside small pieces of meat). Your last night on the horse-hair mattress. In the morning, your last square of chocolate. Your last visit to the back garden. Your last sunlight. Your last pee – you're uncertain on your legs (four too many, it seems, getting all tangled up) and you fall over in slow motion. Your last smell of grass, of moist black earth. Your last glimpse of the two neighbouring cats as they stalk towards us, preying now and unafraid. Your last grooming, the comb sliding through your fur in a wordless goodbye, gathering up a ball of loose golden wool, for me to keep and clutch in my hands, afterwards.

But you don't know any of this. You blame me, us, the world, for not making the pain in your lungs go away. But we will, trust me, we will. When it's too late you'll *know* – trust me this one last time.

Two Ravens Press is the most northerly literary publisher in the UK, operating from a six-acre working croft on a sea-loch in the north-west Highlands of Scotland. Two Ravens Press is run by two writers with a passion for language and for books that are non-formulaic and that take risks. We publish cutting-edge and innovative contemporary fiction, non-fiction and poetry.

Visit our website for comprehensive information on all of our books and authors – and for much more:

- browse all Two Ravens Press books by category or by author, and purchase them online, post & packing-free (in the UK, and for a small fee overseas)

- there is a separate page for each book, including summaries, extracts and reviews, and author interviews, biographies and photographs

- read our daily blog about life as a small literary publisher in the middle of nowhere – or the centre of the universe, depending on your perspective – with a few anecdotes about life down on the croft thrown in. Includes regular and irregular columns by guest writers – Two Ravens Press authors and others.

www.tworavenspress.com